Raylene's Daughter
A Novel

Karen Pless Gaines

ISBN: 978-0-578-97322-7

This book is dedicated to my wonderful grandson, Parker Sonny Ray Espinoza. This past year has been a hard year; I was ready to give up. But, then you my sweet boy, came into my life and breathed a fresh air of determination into this new Gigi.
I love you to the moon and beyond!!

ACKNOWLEDGMENTS

First and foremost, I thank Jesus Christ my savior for the gift of salvation that was given to me freely. If it weren't for His love and mercy, I wouldn't be here today. Many thanks to my family and friends that keep pushing me to write, if it weren't for them, this book would probably still be just a thought. To my husband, Kevin, thank you for supplying me with a place I can go and be alone to write, I love my new office! Kiara, my sweet daughter, thank you for continuing to be a sounding board for my ideas and helping me come up with new ones. To my son, Preston, thanks for helping me with all my computer issues…without you I'd be lost in the sea of technology. And at last, I can never forget to thank all the people who continue to doubt and try to convince me it's not possible, (even on book three), you all keep proving Philippians 4:13 true repeatedly…

I can do all things through Christ who strengthened me.

PRELUDE

Ten days, which is how long he has been here. Ten days of having to climb on that top bunk. His roommate just left for home; now, he has it all to himself. He looks around the seven-by-twelve cell as he finishes making the bottom bunk. If this is going to be his home for the next five years, he sure didn't want to spend it climbing on the top bunk. Should he get another roommate, that's where he would put them, let them climb for a while.

Trevor Sullivan closes his eyes as he envisions the farm back home. Oh, how he misses his comfortable bed and his mama's cooking. He misses more than just her cooking; he misses all of her. The way she would smile up at him from the flower bed as she pulled out the weeds, or the way she would kiss his forehead as she placed a hot plate of food in front of him at the table. He misses his dad and Brenda too, but not like he misses his mama.

Suddenly, visions of tears streaming down her face plays on the backs of his eyelids. He shakes his head and opens his eyes in an attempt to remove that image from his memory, but it's carved there forever. In a few months, he will turn nineteen. In those nineteen years, he has never seen his mama as upset as she was when that judge gave the sentencing, "Five Years in a state penitentiary."

I was trying to get back at dad; I never meant to hurt you, mama, he thought as he squeezed his eyes shut to stop a tear that was trying to escape. Prison is not the place for a man to be crying. Why his dad had to push him to do all those bad things, he will never understand. *Why can't he just let me live my own life? Always telling me, 'You have to learn all this stuff boy, this farm will be yours one day.' I don't want the farm to be mine. I want out of that town.* He gives a low huff of a laugh as he opens his eyes and looks around him, "I guess the joke is on me this time ole man." Trevor stretches out on the bunk and lays his head back on the wall, "Yep, looks like I got my wish," he mutters to the empty room. "I am a hundred miles away from home, living in a cold empty cell. Bet you're happy now."

"Who you talking to man?"

Trevor bolted upright and sat on the edge of the bunk as he gazes at the big burly man at the door. "You haven't been here long enough to go crazy—or were you crazy when you came in?"

Trevor feels himself getting angry and knows this isn't the place to be letting his temper control him; so, he just smiles and shakes his head, "Just thinking about home, man."

"Aren't we all? Come on let's go eat, kid."

He had been so caught up in thoughts that he hadn't heard

the call to go eat, at least he isn't retained to his cell twenty-four seven. However, he keeps to himself most of the time.

Once they were seated, his focus is on the food and home. Eating here makes him miss home more, this food isn't even close to his mama's cooking.

"I've seen you around, but you never talk to anyone—why is that?" the man sitting beside him asked. Trevor only shrugs in response.

"Look, man, I'm not your enemy. I can tell by looking at ya that you are just a kid—you gonna need a friend in here—believe me. And as scared as you look—" the man shakes his head and laughs as he lets his words trail off.

"Who can I get drugs from in here?" Trevor whispers without taking his eyes off the plate in front of him.

The man laughs, "Yeah—you are definitely green—don't be using that word in here—let's start with names—I'm Charlie Banconfield—people in here call me Bacon."

Trevor shakes his outreached hand without looking at him, "Trevor." He finishes swallowing the food that is in his mouth before adding, "Sullivan."

"No nickname?"

"Nope—just Trevor."

"I'll call you Sully then."

"What's wrong with calling me Trevor?"

"A nickname makes you look tougher."

"Whatever suits you dude." Trevor shoves more

food into his mouth while wishing this guy would leave him to his thoughts.

"You missing home—am I right?"

"To repeat what you told me—aren't we all?"

Bacon's belly shook as he let out a rumbling laugh, "You're a fast learner—I think I'm going to like you."

Trevor pushes his plate back in frustration and glares at the old man, "Okay, you win—what do you want to know about me? Do I miss home? Yes—Why? This food sucks and—I miss my family—Why am I here? I beat up my girlfriend and almost killed her—Is there anything else you want to know?"

"You really do need a friend to talk to—were does all this anger come from? You upset that mama couldn't get you out of this one?"

"Leave my mama out of this, man." Trevor pushes the chair back just as Bacon pulls him back up to the table.

"Chill, kid—that type of behavior will get you in a world of trouble, "he whispers to the kid, "believe me when I say—you do not want to draw attention to yourself in here."

"I just want to be left alone—" he rises with his tray in hand, "For now anyway." He walks away before Bacon can reply.

Back in his cell, Trevor stretches out once more on his bunk. For the first time since he was fifteen, he regrets all the decisions he has made. Up until then, he had been an upstanding kid. Getting up at the crack of dawn to help his dad on the farm before leaving for school, straight-A honor roll student despite these chores, and of course, he was the one on his baseball team with the most home runs.

Then the argument with his dad—that's what changed things. His dad managed to take care of over a hundred head of cattle, repair roofs, fix the tractor, along with the other responsibilities of running a cattle farm. Plus, he was the best police officer in McCaysville, Georgia. Yet, he opposed him having dreams about going to college and leaving small-town-Georgia, for a better life.

It wasn't the going to college part that heated things up; it was the fact that Trevor wanted nothing to do with the farm or McCaysville after graduating high school. *'Why can't you just be a cop like me and tend to the farm?'* he had asked. To his dad, this meant the discussion was over. It was settled, Trevor would become a police officer and take over the farm. That's when he had started doing things just to get back at his dad—he would make the ole man beg him to leave.

Trevor started hanging with the rough crowd. Doing drugs and sneaking out to get drunk, stealing things to get the drugs and alcohol, skipping school; you name it—he did it. Even got him put in juvie a couple of times. The boy he once was would have never done all those things—much less beat up a woman. He had been raised in a Christian home from the time he was born. The family had nightly bible reading and discussions; his actions went against everything he had been taught.

Feeling trapped in a town—on a farm—taking on a career he had no interest in, Trevor figured going against those beliefs would help him get out of that small town and find freedom. *It got me out of McCaysville*, he thinks, as he looks around the tiny cell he would call home for the next five years, *but it took my freedom.*

Three years later...

"Haven't you done enough damage?" Brenda blocks the doorway of her father's room, "Can't you ever think of anyone but yourself? You have spent the last seven years in and out of juvie, two times now you have been in prison for beating up two different women and now—" her words trail off as she shakes her head, "—I have lost my mama because of you and—my daddy is lying here fighting for his life—because of you. Just go Trevor—leave and don't come back."

Trevor drops his head at his sister's words. "I only want to tell him I'm sorry Brenda—please let me have that much."

"No! You don't deserve a chance to—what were thinking Trevor?" Tears stream down her face. "You should have known not to get behind the wheel of that car—how much did you have to drink?" she continues without giving him a chance to respond, "All they ever did was love you, but you insisted on doing your own thing, are you happy now?"

"I never meant for anyone to get hurt, Brenda, I swear."

"Just leave, Trevor—and never come back." She walks into her father's hospital room and closes the door, not giving him a chance to speak.

Trevor stands there a few seconds, staring at the door. He has really messed up this time—someone had died because of his actions, and another may be added to that one—two murders; he was sure to never see the outside of prison bars for this one. Then, turning slowly, he walks back down the long hallways, taking the elevator downstairs, and walks outside to his favorite spot on the bench in the garden area.

What is he going to do now? He doesn't want to go back to prison; it has only been a few months since he was released. Suddenly, he hears crying on the other side of an azalea bush that is separating the benches. Standing slowly, he walks around the bush to find a young lady sitting there.

"Are you alright, miss?"

The girl wipes at her tears and straightens as if trying to hide that she was crying. "Nothing—everything—" she stammers in response.

"You want to talk about it?" Trevor offers while taking a seat beside her.

"There really isn't much to talk about—" she lowers her head once again, "My dad is dying—the doctors just told my mom and me that he only has a few days—if that—" the sobbing returns before she continues, "I don't want to lose my daddy."

"Parents are the one thing that is really hard to let go of—do you have other family here?"

She shakes her head no, "We live about two hours from here—it's just me and mom."

"I will be your friend while you are here—if you

7

want—what your name?"

"That would be nice—my name is Raylene."

Chapter 1
The Nightmare Begins

She doesn't look back as she runs out of the house and down the street. For the first time since they moved into this neighborhood, Raylene Sullivan is thankful they live within walking distance to downtown. Except she doesn't walk, she runs as fast as her feet will take her. Is he behind her? The last time she had seen him is when she had rolled him off her after smashing the vase upside his head. Is he dead? She didn't know or care at this moment, getting away from him is all she can think about.

Hot liquid streams down her forehead into her eyes. The stinging causing them to tear so bad she can hardly see where she is going. The thin nightshirt she wears did little to protect her from the cold frigid air, but she doesn't seem to notice. The frozen concrete cuts into her bare feet, there was no time for shoes as she left the house. Survival is the only thing on her mind.

The stores up ahead are dark, as she searches frantically for a light on in any window at all. Raylene grasps at the handles, hoping to find one unlocked. Finally, she spots the Quick Mart on the corner. For the first time since she ran out of her home she screams as she runs across the street and into the store. "Help Me! Somebody please...Help me!" she leans across the counter, leaving blood smears over the clean, white surface. "He's going to kill me...Please help me!"

The clerk behind the counter looks at the strange person who has just barged into his store. Her face is drenched in blood, he isn't sure where it's coming from, but he quickly looks her over from head to toe. He notices she is clutching her abdomen; the spot is saturated with blood. Adrenaline quickly kicks in and he grabs the gun he keeps under the counter, runs out into the parking lot, and searches to see if this wounded lady had been followed. Not seeing anyone, he goes back into the store, and locks the door behind him. Taking Raylene by the arm, he pulls her into the office, out of sight from anyone who may come searching for her. He pulls the chair away from the desk and leads her to it, "Ma'am, can you tell me what happened?" he asks as he dials 911.

"My husband...my husband..." she stammered between gaps, "Please help me...my baby," she adds as she looks down at the blood gushing through her nightshirt.

The clerk speaks quickly, "Please hurry, she looks bad, and I think she's pregnant."

"Please save my baby." she wheezes out as her body goes limp and she slides from the chair to the floor.

****

Raylene blinks, trying to open her eyes against the lights bright beam. *Someone shut off that light,* her brain screams the words, but she cannot seem to get her mouth to work. "I think she's coming around," she hears a female voice say. She blinks again and tries to focus past the light at the fuzzy outline of a person. Who is this? Where is she and how did she get here?

"Can you tell me your name?" the female shadow asks. Raylene just can't get her eyes to focus. "Who did this to you? Can you tell us what happened?" the shadow asks. Then suddenly it all starts coming back to her. Where is Kurt? Is he here? Nylah! Where is Nylah?

"Ny…lah," she manages to whisper over and over, "Nylah." Her mind races to remember those last moments before everything went black. She had told Kurt she wanted a divorce. She had told him she was taking Nylah, and they were going back to Georgia. Kurt had gone into a rage and… *the knife…*he had a knife. She tries to sit up and look at her stomach, but the tubes and wires, along with the meds, won't let her move. *He tried to kill me…*her mouth tries to scream but all she can say is, "Nylah."

"Nylah? Is that your name?" the shadow asks. Raylene fights hard against the blackness she feels overtaking her once again. She needs to get up…she doesn't have time to go back to sleep. Nylah needs her.

"The store clerk had mentioned she might be pregnant," she hears another voice…a male this time, "that was proven not to be the case…could she be talking about a baby she already has?" the male voice whispers.

"That would be terrible." She hears the female voice whisper back. "That means whoever did this has her." Raylene can hear the panic in her voice. She must find a way to tell them. *Stay awake Raylene…fight!*

"No…get Nylah." Raylene manages to say as she fights the darkness of sleep. "He has her…please save my baby."

"He who? Tell us who has Nylah." the female voice urges an answer. "Say his name…come on…just say it," the woman pleads as reality begins to dawn in her mind, "Someone tried to kill this woman and now they have her child."

"Kurt," Raylene whispers as she gives into the darkness and is once again asleep.

"Kurt?" the woman repeats to her partner, "Get a search started on every man named Kurt…push this ahead of everything…I want to find the Kurt who did this to her." she says vehemently as she points towards Raylene. "Liam, we have to find this child…now!" her whisper is barely audible as she adds, "before it's too late…if it's not already."

"I'm ahead of you, I've texted an urgent message to all stations around this area," he squeezes his partner's shoulders as he passes her and heads towards the door, "We'll find her…I promise."

****

Raylene jumps as she comes awake. She opens her eyes to a mostly dark room, only a small stream of light is coming through a doorway off to the left of the room; *It must be a bathroom,* she thinks to herself. The noise that had stolen her from her sleep sounds again to the right of the bed. Raylene turns to see a person sitting in the bedside chair, head propped in an awkward position against the wall. She looks this clean, crisp woman up and down. Although her mouth is open, allowing drool to seep down her chin, Raylene can tell she is an intelligent, professional person by the way that her starched, white shirt remains tucked in her belted slacks, even in her slumped position. The lady's auburn, shoulder length hair is a rumpled mess, Raylene guesses, that it too, was once as put together as the rest of this slender, petite woman. As far as she knows she has never seen this woman before.

Voices in the hallway snaps Raylene's attention back to the other side of the room. *There's that male voice I heard earlier. Who is he?* Raylene thinks to herself, just as the woman beside the bed stirs once again. "Oh, you're awake," the woman says with a warm smile. "Do you need me to get a nurse? Are you okay?" Raylene just stares at her as if she has spoken a foreign language.

She doesn't hear the door open and is startled when the voice from the hallway echoes the woman's words, "You're awake," he walks slowly to her bedside as if expecting her to attack. "You want me to get the nurse?"

"She just asked me the same thing," Raylene points to the woman in the chair, "But, I don't think so. Do I look like I need a nurse?" She looks from one side of the bed to the other at each of the strangers.

"Do you feel okay?" the man leans in towards her, "You want me to adjust your pillows for you?"

Raylene glances back to the pillows behind her, "I don't know, do they look like they need to be adjusted?" At this point she has begun to like this little back-n-forth, awkward game they were playing. She takes in the man before her, although he is dressed in the same white shirt, black slacks as the woman, wrinkles don't seem to bother him. His disheveled apparel doing little to hide the ruggedly muscular body underneath. His tousled hair, the color reminding Raylene of a wheatfield, seemingly intensifies the steely blue of his eyes. His immense stature makes him seem to tower over her as he approaches the bedside.

"D...do you need anything?" he stutters, as he reaches the edge of her bed.

Raylene recoils from his outreached hand, "Names would be a good start." she looks from one to the other, "and why are you here?"

"We are really sorry about that," the woman begins as she rises from the chair, "I am Detective River Donaldson." she offers with an outreached hand, "but you can call me River."

Raylene ignores the hand as she turns to look up at the towering man on the other side of the bed. "You are?"

"Liam...Detective Liam Geoffrey." He doesn't offer his hand to Raylene; he instead turns to pull a chair to the side of the bed. "We have been waiting for you to wake up. Can you tell us who you are and who did this to you?"

"Why should I trust you?" Raylene sinks back into the pillows and looks from one detective to the other. "You're one of them."

River's confusion was obvious as she looks towards her partner, "One of who?" she asks Raylene.

"You asked who did this to me…" Raylene sits straight up in bed, "Lieutenant Kurt Sullivan…that's who; but my guess is that you two already know that. Did he send you here?"

"No, he didn't." Liam offers confused. "Like my partner mentioned…we have been waiting on you to wake up and tell us who did this," he leans in slightly, "and to find Nylah."

Raylene bolts from the bed, "How do you know Nylah? Where is she…do you have her?" she yanks at the wires and tubes connected to her arm, "Get this off me!" she yells towards the door that leads out to the hallway.

"Miss, calm down…" River reaches out to her soothingly. "You need to calm down, you don't want to rip open the sutures on your abdomen."

Raylene glances down towards the stab wounds. Hugging herself tightly as she walks back and sits on the edge of the bed, "Please tell me she's alright…and Kurt?" she looks up at both detectives who are now standing in front of her, "Is he.... alive?

"Ma'am, we don't know anything, because up until just now…we only knew two first names…and that's not much to go on," Liam runs a hand through the rumpled mop on his head, "Can you tell us who you are?"

"Like you don't already know." Raylene doesn't try to hide the venom in her words, "everybody knows who Lieutenant Kurt Sullivan is around here...or a version of him that doesn't exist, nobody but me and Nylah knows who he is behind closed doors, and..."

"Are you his wife?" River interrupts.

Raylene pushes the button for the nurse, "I'm not going to play this game with you!" She yells to the two detectives.

A female voice booms through the intercom on the wall above the bed, "Can I help you?" "Please come remove these unwanted guests from my room." She responds, never taking her eyes off the detectives.

"Mrs. Sullivan, we only want to help you." River trying hard to gain this battered and bruised woman's trust.

"I never said I was his wife, now did I?" Raylene replies through clenched teeth. Just then the door opens as a blonde nurse walks into the room, "Good-bye detectives and please do not come back."

She watches the two of them exit the room with the nurse right behind them. She can hear mumbles in the hallway as they spoke. Finally, the echo of their footsteps fade as they walk away. Raylene is still staring at the closed door when the blonde nurse returns pushing a cart with a computer on top with a blood pressure monitor attached to a pole extended above it.

The nurse smiles warmly as she walks towards the bed, "Hi, it's good to see you awake and doing so well," she reaches over the head of the bed and turns the overhead light on, "My name is Bella, I'm the RN on duty tonight. I just want to check your vitals and get some information from you…if that's okay." Raylene just nods but offers nothing more as she extends her arm as the nurse wraps the blood pressure cuff around it. "Vitals look good," the nurse smiles as she pulls the cart so that the computer is in front of her. "I need to put in some information on you…okay?" Bella glances towards Raylene who still only answers with a nod. "Can you tell me your name?"

"Raylene Abyelah Sullivan." Raylene offers, "Wife of Lieutenant Kurt Sullivan. He's the one who did this to me." The nurse gives a weak smile as Raylene speaks, "I figured that was going to be your next question," Raylene returns the nurse's smile.

They spent the next few minutes filling in all the blanks, even the part where Kurt was unmoving on the floor as she ran from the house to get away from him. When the questions are all finished, the nurse walks towards the bed with a syringe in hand, "This will help you rest for the night." The nurse is saying as she inserts it into Raylene's IV port. The room starts to spin before the syringe is even empty, then… the world is dark again.

****

The blood pounds in her ears, her heart thuds in her chest, her hands shake, her feet tingle. Her vision is disfigured, as if she were looking through a kaleidoscope. She must get away, but how? Kurt's weight on top of her keeps her pinned to the floor. Raylene pushes harder, and wiggles, finally she pulls herself free. A loud crash behind her causes her to turn, *who's there!* She screams in her mind, but her mouth won't work. She sits there on the floor paralyzed by the fear that courses through her. A shuffling noise in the darkness draws her attention once more, "Who-who's there?" She manages weakly. But no answer is given. Slowly Raylene begins to wake up. *It was only a dream.* She breathes a sigh of relief just as she hears the shuffle beside her bed, someone is there. Raylene thinks, *but who?* She fights hard against the drug-induced sleep to open her eyes; a blurry figure appears before her.

"Did I wake you?" the figure whispers.

Kurt! Oh no! Kurt is here, scream Raylene...scream loud! She urges herself on, but no words will come, she feels paralyzed as she watches the figure hold her IV line and uncap a syringe with his teeth. She can't make out his features, but she knows his voice well.

"Don't worry darlin', you'll be back to sleep in no time," Kurt sneers down at her, "this time for good...I want my version of the story told, not yours, your story could ruin everything for me. I can't have that version being told."

Raylene tries hard to make herself scream, she pleads with her eyes for him to stop, "Nylah," she manages to say.

"Nylah will be just fine darlin', I'll find someone to raise that kid of yours, I'm sure." Kurt could never pass up an opportunity to let her know how much he detested her having a baby, and now was no different. He acts as if she created the child all by herself, and that he had no part in it. "Now, go night, night sweetie." He gives an eval laugh just as he sticks the needle into the port.

"Help Me," Raylene tries to scream but it comes out as just a whisper. "Please, no." she pleads once more with her husband. She closes her eyes in helpless abandon just as the door to her room burst open. She opens her eyes but sees nothing, her eyes refusing to focus on anything clearly. A tall figure grabs Kurt, knocking the syringe to the floor before he can insert the med in the line. They disappear from her view, but she can hear them shuffling about on the floor. A male voice screaming out in pain...*Detective Geoffrey? What is he doing here?* Finally, the shuffling stops and one of the figures run from the room. Then everything goes quiet.

Raylene shakenly pushes the button for the nurse, "Kurt was in my room," she begins frantically, "then Detective Geoffrey came in, they were fighting, and one of them may be dead on my floor, please hurry!" she leans slightly, trying to see who is on the floor, just as a hand appears on the railing.

"I'm alright." Detective Geoffrey says through huffs of air. "Just trying to catch my breath." Raylene jumps as he pulls himself up. "I'm sorry, I didn't mean to frighten you."

"What are you doing here?" she asks just as her doorway is flooded by cops. Liam waves them off, "I thought I told you not to come back?" Raylene continues.

Liam sat on the chair, bending down to pick up the empty syringe on the floor, "I was on my way home from the office and thought I would stop by and check on you. If I hadn't," he waves the syringe in the air, "This would have been in you."

"It's empty, so how do you know it's not?" Raylene says with a sneer.

"Because it's in my bullet proof vest," he interjects as he opens his shirt to reveal a wet circle on his vest. "I'm only trying to help you Mrs. Sullivan."

"Raylene," she mumbles.

"I'm sorry...what?" Liam leans closer.

"My name is Raylene...I don't like to be called Mrs. Sullivan." She gives a half smile.

"Okay, Raylene...you can call me Liam...I don't like to be called Detective Geoffrey" He returns her smile before continuing, "Will you let me help you...please?" he extends his hand hoping she will take it.

Raylene stares blankly at the hand in front her, she trusts no one, but she could really use someone on her side, that is the only way she is ever going to find her daughter. "Okay...but tomorrow. I'm exhausted and could really use some sleep." Her smile is wide as she shakes his hand in agreement.

Liam returns her smile, "Well, you get some sleep, and I'll go deal with these guys" he nods towards the band of cops still standing in her doorway, "Good-night Raylene." He adds as he walks towards the door.

"Good-night Liam" she returns, as she watches the door close behind him.

Chapter 2
Liam

Detective Liam Geoffrey hovers over his desk. After leaving the hospital he called Ronny, the Chief of police, and filled him in on his findings. They had been watching Lieutenant Sullivan for a while now. However, he had not told Raylene that her husband was the reason he was in Chicago. He hadn't mentioned that no one on the force was aware that Kurt had a wife, much less a kid. He couldn't help but wonder if Raylene knew that her husband was suspected of running a drug and prostitution ring. If she did, she hadn't mentioned it. She had only talked about him hardly being at home and the abuse that happened when he *was* there.

In a few hours he must go tell this, already distraught woman that upon searching her home it seems as if Kurt is on the run with her daughter. When he and Ronny arrived at her house, they found the front door wide open. Signs of a struggle was evident throughout the living room. A pool of blood, which they assumed was a mixture of both Raylene and Kurt's, was near a broken vase in the center of the room. Drops of blood was also found going up the stairs into the master bedroom, then trailed to what appeared to be Nylah's room; blood stains on the dressers and clothes in the closet showed signs that he had took essentials that would be needed when he fled the scene.

He had taken pictures of the scene while he was there, now they lay spread out over his desk in front of him. He looked at each one, trying to piece together the events that took place that night. By the looks of things, Raylene must have put up a good fight for such a small woman. Although not as petite as River, she couldn't weigh much over 125 pounds. Kurt loved to flaunt and flex his gym-induced muscle around the station from what Ronny had told him. A woman Raylene's size wouldn't hold much of a chance up against someone like that, and now that monster was out there somewhere with that innocent little girl.

He picks up the picture of Kurt, staring into his dark eyes, "What are your plans?" Liam voices out loud, "and you better not hurt that little girl." The smile Kurt wore seems to mock Liam. Never in his life had he ever felt so frustrated. Never had he wanted to get his hands on someone as bad as he wants to get them on Kurt. Ronny had called him back in November and asked for a favor. Said he had a cop that was rumored to be dirty; and he needed a face no one in Chicago would recognize to catch this dirt-bag.

He had been driving by Kurt's house that night when the commotion at the Quick Mart caught his eye. He had no idea that the woman they were putting into the back of the ambulance was Kurt Sullivan's wife. If only he had known, he would have gone back to the house, Kurt would no doubt still be there; Raylene would still have her daughter, and they would have Kurt behind bars where he belongs. Just then the phone beside him rings, Liam reaches to answer it.

"Detective Geoffrey, how—" he began, "River… slow down…I understand that you have a lot to do Tod— …no family whatsoever...uh-huh…continue looking into that, I'll touch base with you later today…bye." Liam scratched his head as he places the phone back on the desk. How can a man be a lieutenant and no information be found on him? Kurt Sullivan was getting more mysterious every day.

He reaches for the phone just as it rings again, "River—…Hi Ronny, I was just about to call—, WHAT…I'll meet you in the northside parking dock…did you call the hospital security…let them know that jerk could be on the grounds." He hangs up and darts for the door. *If he touches her again, I promise I will kill him this time.*

****

Liam is breathing hard by the time he reaches Raylene's door. *That's odd why is it open and the bed made?* His heart races as he realizes what happened. "When did Mrs. Sullivan get released, and how long has she been gone?" he yells at the nurse passing by him in the hallway.

"About ten minutes—"

Liam didn't give her time to finish. He runs back towards the elevator as he takes his phone from his back pocket, "Ronny…Raylene has been released…no, she has left already…I'm heading over there now," he disconnects the call as he pushes the button on the elevator. Once inside he tries to phone River, when she doesn't answer he leaves her a brief message of what is happening and tells her to be on the lookout for Kurt. He places the phone back in his pocket and leans against the door of the elevator. *How long does it take to get to the ground floor?* He grumbles silently.

He darts out the door as soon as it opens and races to his car. He must get to her house before something bad happens to her. *God, please don't let Kurt be there. Let Raylene be safe…why didn't she let someone know she was being released? She should not be going there alone…how did she get there?* That last thought makes him pause as his heartrate quickens. He had failed to ask who picked her up…did she take a cab? His mind was racing just as fast as his car.

Liam blares the horn as he swerves out into traffic, the other cars respond in the same fashion. Chicago winters always make travel almost impossible, but he pays the snow no mind as he pushes past the waiting traffic and flies across the intersection. Traffic from left and right braking hard. One car dents the back of another, tires are screeching, Liam doesn't seem to see the traffic at all, his mind is set on one thing…getting to Raylene before Kurt does. He spots her road up ahead on the right, traffic is moving steady with no break for him to change lanes; he races faster to move ahead of the cars beside him and with a quick jerk makes the right-hand turn in front of the line, sliding sideways onto the road, the car swerves as he fights the wheel to get it under control. Never slowing his speed, he jerks the wheel as he turns into the second driveway on the right, the car sliding to a stop as he slams on the brakes in her front yard.

It's hard to tell if anyone is here at this time of the day. The sunlight on the melting snow making it impossible to tell if there were lights on inside the house. Liam throws the car in park and darts for the front door which he finds open about an inch. He knows that he and Ronny had secured the place when they left that night. Surely, she would not have left the door open, she knows that Kurt is on the loose.

Unarmed he enters the house slowly and calls Raylene's name. He searches the entire first floor before taking the stairs to the upper level; still calling out her name…no answer. Except for the front door being open, there is no sign of her ever being here. *Raylene, where did you go? Was he here when you returned? What about family?* With that last thought he makes a call to River. He is hoping she would have some answers.

"Hey, did you do a search on Raylene…no…okay do one now…I'm at the house now…no she's not…that's what I want to find out…let me know what you find on her…bye.

He walks out the door, making sure to lock it as he leaves. On the way back to his car he looks at the snow, there are no tire tracks nor fresh footprints outside of his, so who ever went into the house did it before last night's fresh snow fall, and no one had been there today. He climbed into his car and started the engine, going back to the hospital…the last place Raylene was seen… seemed like the best place to start.

****

Liam unlocks the door to their make-shift office. Ronny had apologized for the rough condition it was in, as he explained that this was the best he could find on such short notice. It was once a storage room for the abandoned restaurant that sat adjacent to it. The two battered desked that sat touching, facing each other had been donated from the thrift shop across the street. Two wabbly chairs sit at each, there isn't any room for much more, but at least it gives River and him a place to work and keep track of paperwork they have collected.

River is gazing intently at the papers strewed out over her desk, when Liam walks into the room. "Hiya" she turns to smile up to him, "I was wondering when you would get here…I have coffee," she points to the take-out cup sitting on his desk.

"How long have you been here?" he asks as he pulls his chair out and plops down.

"I got here…ohm…about 9 o'clock last night," she stretches back in her chair and yawns.

"You've been here all night?"

"yep"

"Then please tell me you have figured out Kurt's location."

"Nope."

Liam realizes this was going nowhere. River is the type of person who just won't say much when she is mulling over things in her mind. His best route was to just start with what he knew at this point, then maybe she would jump in with what she has.

"I spent most of the night staking out Raylene's house, she never came home last night." He then starts from the beginning when he got the call from Ronny that Kurt, or someone who looks like Kurt, was seen in the hospital parking lot, he got there to discover Raylene had been released, but didn't go home. "I went back to the hospital, they said she called a cab. But we don't know where the cab driver took her."

"Didn't you ask the driver?" River never looks up from the papers she is studying in front of her.

"Yes…he won't tell us anything, said Raylene told him not too."

River peers up at him, "Didn't you tell him who you were and why we needed to—"

"Yes, I did," Liam's frustration can be heard in his voice, "He said she made him promise not to tell anyone, especially the police."

"We're not the police."

"I know, I told—"

"Liam! How can we protect her if we don't know where she is?"

"I know—"

"Is all you can say is '*I know*'?" River rises from her seat and storms from the room.

Liam dashes from his chair and follows her out the door. "River, what do you want me to say? I'm just as frustrated as you are right now…I want to protect her…I want to find Kurt and Nylah before it's too late."

"Then act like it!" River screams at him as she turns and walks up the sidewalk.

Liam didn't follow her this time; he knows how she is when she gets like this. The only thing to do is to let her walk it off. "She should have at least grabbed her jacket." Liam shivered as he heads back into the office. He has no idea what his next move will be. He has searched everywhere he thought she might go; the shelters in town, the park, he keeps calling the hospital just in case she went back there, he watched her house all night. "Raylene, where did you go?" He must find a way to get that cab driver to talk. Raylene's safety depends on it.

Chapter 3

Raylene

Raylene blinks against the bright rays of sunlight that beams through the crack in the curtains across the room. She lays there, motionless, staring at the window. Her mind still focused on Nylah. Where would Kurt be hiding with her? Her thoughts drift back to when she had first met Kurt, just nine short years earlier.

It was the summer she graduated high school. Her dad was struggling with stage four Hodgkin's Disease and was being sent to Emory Hospital for treatment. Her parents decided that it would be best to rent an apartment in Atlanta rather than make trips back and forth.

Raylene hated being there. Atlanta was a big contrast to the Blue Ridge life she was used to. It has never been clear as to what Kurt was doing there that summer. Raylene had bumped into him a few times in the hallway when she would be on her way to or from her dad's room. One day he decided to speak to her. After that he acted like they were old friends who had always known each other. Then, two nights before she was to start her freshman year at college, Kurt asked her out on a date. That's the night that changed the course of her life forever.

She had always planned on going to University of Georgia. Kurt didn't like that idea. He said she should go to the University of Illinois in Chicago. Of course, she had went on with her plans for freshman year. But by her sophomore year, Kurt had talked her into transferring. By that time, her dad had lost his battle with that horrible disease, and her mom was back home in Blue Ridge. Raylene felt that getting away for a while would be the best for her at this time. So, she had taken Kurt up on his offer.

Within a month, they were married…a private ceremony of course. That's when things changed for the worse. She never got to finish her teaching degree…never even stepped foot inside the university. Then, five years later she found out she was pregnant. Raylene's life really spiraled into despair with that news. She had thought Kurt would be thrilled with the news. Instead, he was furious. Demanding that she abort the baby, saying he did not want children, now or ever. Raylene made the choice to have the baby against his wishes. Kurt never acknowledged the child.

Raylene had hired a nanny to keep the baby away when Kurt was home. This choice was made when he threatened to kill the child if he ever saw or heard it while he was there. What had happened to the happy-go-lucky guy she met at the hospital? He seemed to disappear overnight. She had asked about his family a few times and was demanded never to mention them again.

Kurt was never an easy person to read or to get information out of. Just like he had always avoided her question about who he had at the hospital, he did the same when she had asked where he was from. Answering only that he lived in Chicago. He never mentioned family, called them, or visited any in the last eight years. She only knew that his name was Kurt Daniel Sullivan, who became Lieutenant Kurt Daniel Sullivan six years after they met. At that time, they had been married nearly five years; and Nylah was due any day. The guys at the station threw a party to celebrate, Raylene wasn't allowed to go. Kurt always told her that he wanted no one to know about her to keep her safe, but the other officers didn't seem to keep their families secret to protect them. Why did she have to remain a secret?

The worst beating she ever received was when she had gone to the station unannounced. Nylah was very sick, and she couldn't reach the private doctor that Kurt had hired to make house calls. Which so happened to be the same doctor that delivered Nylah at home. He always said that the things he did was to keep them safe and yet she just kept putting them in danger. What danger? Who did they need protection from? Kurt was the only one hurting them.

Raylene shakes her head to clear her thoughts as she pushes the covers back and slowly sits up, pain coursing through her abdomen with each move. She slowly rises from the bed and walks over to the window and pushes open the curtain. She was thankful that Mrs. Johnson let her use the guest room last night. The Johnsons are the only people she knows in this neighborhood. It is kind of funny if you think about it, a place as big as Chicago, and yet they are the only people Raylene ever met.

She peers across the street at the huge house she called home for the past eight years. As a child growing up in a small town, this was the sort of place she dreamed of living in one day. The property boasts of tall oak trees and a well-groomed lawn with professionally installed flower gardens. A gazebo stands off to the far side of the front lawn, it's white paint glistening in the morning sunlight. All of it a delightful framework for the towering mass of concrete, stonework, and wood siding, that makes up the exterior of their home. It looks like a happy place, a place that promises calmness and peace to all that enter through its doors. Raylene shutters as the memories of that night flood her thoughts. She closes her eyes to block them out. If those walls could talk, they would tell of a life quite opposite of the calmness and peace that the outside portrays.

"Oh, you're up." Mrs. Johnson opens the door and walks inside the room, "I have eggs, bacon, and toast if you would like to come down for breakfast."

"I'm not hungry, thank you though,"

"I'll leave it in the microwave...just in case you change your mind."

Raylene only nods.

"We've got to leave soon to go to the doctors...Is there anything I can do for you? Do you need help getting dressed?

Raylene shakes her head, "No, but thanks for offering." She watches as Mrs. Johnson closes the door behind her, *I probably should have let her help me get dressed. But I'll manage somehow.* She reaches for her clothes which were folded on the table by the bed and starts slowly getting dressed. She doesn't know what her plans for today are but getting across that road is the first.

She thinks about the car she saw there yesterday. She had asked the taxi driver to let her out at the Quick Mart. She wanted to thank the attendant for helping her that night. When she left the store, she spotted a black Dodge Charger in her driveway. Last night she had seen that same car parked up the street, watching and waiting for her to come home no doubt. She has no idea who drives such a car. The cleaning service she had sent to clean up, had called before she left the hospital. She knew they had already left. Had Kurt sent someone there looking for her...was it Kurt himself. He has a lot of friends, maybe he had borrowed a car that no one would recognize. Not knowing who it is, or if they would be back, she had decided to walk to the Johnsons' and ask to stay here.

The car was gone now, she presses her face against the window to allow her to see up the street. She walks back to the bed and makes it as best she can, laying the shirt neatly across the foot. She makes her way downstairs. The house is quiet, so she knows the Johnsons have already left. The frigid air feels like pins on her face as she walks out the front door. She knows right away that the snow is going to cause a problem for her, there are no footprints or tracks in her yard. She has no choice; she needs clothes and essentials to live on; and the money she keeps hid from Kurt behind the water heater.

Raylene had started hiding back money as often as she could, shortly after Nylah was born. She had finally saved enough to get the two of them back to Georgia. They would be there by now if Kurt hadn't come home early that night and caught her packing a suitcase. Her mom was going to pick them up at the airport in Atlanta. "Mom! Oh no!" Raylene caps her hand over her mouth as the words echo through the air, "She must be frantic, wondering what happened to us," she adds…with a whisper this time.

Raylene starts across the street as fast as the snow, and the pain that is coursing through her body will let her go. Shakenly, she reaches to move the flowerpot beside the front door. "Good…it's still here," she says, as she reaches for the key and unlocks the door. She quietly walks inside, what if someone is here? Raylene feels like a ninja as she slips silently inside the door. She quickly scans the living and dining room, the kitchen is out of sight, so she makes a quick glance up the stairs and removes her shoes and sets them down slowly by the door. She then tiptoes towards the kitchen, the only sound she can hear is the blood pounding through her head as her heart races.

Once she clears the kitchen, she goes to the counter, taking a knife from the stand near the stove. Using the same ninja moves she makes her way up the stairs. Once on the landing she moves towards Nylah's room first, no one is there; tears fill her eyes as she looks at her daughter's empty bed. She must keep her emotions in check, she must stay calm to find Nylah. She moves slowly on down the hallway to her bedroom, seeing the closed door makes her heart pound harder. She holds her breath as she walks slowly across the hallway. quietly turning the doorknob, gripping the knife tightly, she raises it as she flings open the door...no one is there. Half relieved and half disappointed, Raylene rushes to the closet to find the suitcase she had packed. She doesn't know where she is going, but she can't stay here.

Taking her cellphone off the charger, she texts her mom a simple message for now, 'I'm fine, I'll call you later.' Shoving the phone into her back pocket, and taking the charger, she starts down the stairs, she suddenly stops dead in her tracks. "What are you doing here? And how did you get in?" Liam is standing in the middle of the living room.

"Th-th-the door was open," he stammers, pointing to the door.

"Get out! Now!" she searches for the knife; she must have left it upstairs. She sees the black car sitting in the driveway, the same black car that has been watching her house.

"Raylene," Liam holds up his hands in surrender, "Please—"

"Please nothing, does he have you watching me?" she points to the car, "I watched you most of the night, sitting and waiting on me to come home."

"You've got it all wrong, Raylene"

Raylene takes a step towards him, hoping to back him out the door. She doesn't trust this man, or anyone affiliated with the police. Kurt is always good at sucking people in. He always seems to have a way of making people like him, a way of making himself look like a saint. Why would Detective Liam be any different? Her heart begins to race when Liam doesn't budge from his position. "I don't think I do detective," she hopes she seems confident to him; she prays her nervousness doesn't show, "I think my husband has you watching me to make sure I'm not out looking for him and—" she freezes when the thought strikes her and suddenly, she wants to run, she has to get out of this house, away from these people.

"And what?" Liam is staring at her intently.

"How do I know he didn't send you to get rid of me?" Raylene can hear the shaking of her voice and knows he can too. She in no way wants this man to know how afraid she is. She squares her shoulders, trying to hide the fear racing through her.

"I only want to help you, you're being absurd. I know you are scared, and you don't know who to trust, but I need you to talk to me, so we find Kurt and in doing so, find Nylah." She watches as Liam throws his hands up in exasperation. He almost convinces her into believing him.

Kurt is like that. Easy to make people believe any lie he tells. If Detective Liam was sent by Kurt, then he would know all the right things to say to get her to trust him. She wasn't about to fall for that. She wasn't about to let Kurt win; she is going to find him, even if she has to do it alone. "If you are not sent here by Kurt, then tell me what you know so far, where is he?" she wasn't going to let go of her defiance that easily.

"We've had a few leads, but all of them turned up nothing." Liam runs his hands through his thick locks of hair. "I have people looking into a lead in New York. So far that has turned up empty as well."

"New York?"

"Yes, there was a call that came in, that a car resembling his was followed into New York."

"And" Raylene waves her hand in circles, bidding him to go on.

"No, lost sight of him. They checked around at the hotels and he hasn't checked into any in the area where he was last seen."

"Did you ever stop to think that he probably wouldn't use his real name?" Raylene takes in a deep breath and exhales it loudly, "Cops these days are so stupid…and apparently detectives too." She nods to Liam, as she points toward him. "If you will excuse me, I need to go find my daughter." As she pushes him out the door she adds, "It seems I'm the only one competent enough to do so." She shuts the door in his face ending the conversation.

She peeks out the window just in time to see him get into his car. He is holding the phone to his ear, probably calling Kurt to inform him of what was just said. She knows what she has to do as she runs up the stairs back to her bedroom, she is glad that she had already packed a bag of things she might need. She grabs the bag and goes back down the stairs to the water heater and reaches behind it to retrieve the bag of money she had hid there. Raylene is going to New York to find her daughter.

****

Since arriving in New York, Raylene's experience has been unfavorable, to put it mildly. With the little information she has on Kurt, it is not enough to help locate him. New York is a huge place, and she has no idea what part of New York to search. She assumes it will be near the interstate she and Kurt taken when they had traveled to New York a few times. The search has turned up nothing. She has decided to take the train to the Hampton Inn downtown.

While waiting on the train Raylene has the misfortune of being in the wrong place at the wrong time. The station looks deserted this time of day. A sign on the ticket window states that the attendant will be back in thirty minutes. However, the sign does not say when the attendant left. While propping up against the wall to wait patiently she is mugged. Everything she has with her was in that bag, her identification, her cellphone, and her money.

She remembers the change that she had placed in her jeans pocket when she had bought a sauerkraut dog from a vendor earlier. She uses that to make a call to Liam. Why she would call him of all people, she doesn't have a clue. She can't call her mom and Liam is the only other choice. He doesn't answer, so she leaves him a message telling him where she is and what had happened. She has no way of calling him back, nor does he have a way to call her.

She walks over to the brick building behind the phone booth, hoping to find a way to stop the cold, frigid air that seems to slice right through her. Raylene pulls her sweater tight around her, almost as if she were trying to hide inside it. She backs against the cold brick wall behind her and slides down to the ground, planting her feet in front of her, she hugs her knees against her chest. Sirens blare off in the distance and car horns blast as people on the sidewalk bustle past her. She should have never come here, her only hope is that Liam checks his messages and comes to her rescue. After the way she has treated him, he could decide to leave her to fend for herself, that would be awful. "God, please don't let me die on these dirty streets of New York." She mutters into the sleeve of her sweater.

At some point she dozes off to sleep. She slowly opens her eyes when she thinks she has heard someone say her name. Thinking she is dreaming she gives into the sleepy fog that has overtaken her. Just then Liam bends down to gently nudge her, "The car would be much warmer," he is saying. Thinking he is someone trying to mug her again, she pushes him backwards as she jumps to her feet.

"Get away from me," she shouts as she stands up. Realizing it is Liam she apologizes as she watches him struggle to get his balance.

He laughs as he straightens himself, "Easy, I'm your knight in shining armor, here to rescue you."

Raylene once again hugs her sweater tight around her, "I hope you don't think this means I trust you. I had no one else to call." She walks past him and opens the door to his car, "I bet Kurt was thrilled to hear that I had called you when in trouble." She sits down in the car, slamming the door before he can respond. She watches in the mirror as he walks around to the driver side of the car and gets in.

"I don't know why you won't trust us," he reaches down and snaps his seatbelt in place before putting the car into drive, "we only want to help you."

"We? Who is we?"

"Me and my partner River. That's two people...therefore 'we'"

Raylene stares out the window. She doesn't want to talk to this man beside her. She only wants to get back home. Liam is the first to speak after a long silence. "We've decided...River and I...have decided that it is best if you come stay at her place."

"Not happening."

"Why not?"

"For one…I have a home…two…I don't know either of you or what your intentions are," she turns to face him, "Did Kurt have anything to do with that decision?"

"Why do you keep throwing up Kurt?" Liam shakes his head, "I have no idea what Kurt wants or likes, nor do I care…I only want to find Nylah before he hurts that little girl."

Raylene remains silent.

"I thought you wanted the same thing. But apparently not because all you do is—"

"How dare you say that I don't want to get my daughter out of the hands of that monster!" Raylene feels her face burn with the anger coursing through her.

"Then work with us Raylene." Liam doesn't know what else he could say to this woman to make her understand his intentions are honest. He turns on the radio to drown out the silence in the car. Raylene doesn't seem to want to talk to him, so letting the music fill the space seems better.

"Okay, but we stay at my house, I'd feel more comfortable with that," Raylene turns the music up louder before he could answer.

"I'm sure she wouldn't mind," Liam was smiling as he reaches to turn the radio louder.

Raylene isn't sure how this is going to work out, but it is the only way she can find out what these two are up to. She lays back and closes her eyes. Sleeping will make the trip seem faster.

Chapter 4
River

River brings in the last box of her things. Raylene has set up the guest room downstairs for her. She can see why Raylene doesn't want to stay with her. This house is absolutely beautiful. The kind of house most women would love to call home. Its décor seems to have been done by an interior designer. Even the guest room is eloquently put together. The neutral colors would welcome anyone, it isn't designed to just fit a female's taste. River can tell a lot of thought has gone into every piece of furniture and decoration that is placed here.

"What are you—" Raylene screeches from the living room, bringing River out of her head and back into the moment. "River!"

River rounds the corner, just in time to see Raylene tumble to the floor and a big ball of yellow fur is all River can see. "Dax!" she runs over to rescue Raylene, "Down boy!"

"Is he your…Liam didn't mention you have a dog, if you can even call that thing a dog." Raylene takes the hand River has extended to her, once she is on her feet again, she frantically brushes her clothes back in place.

"I'm—"

"Are you going to explain yourself or not!"

River feels her face burn hot. She had thought Liam told Raylene about Dax. "I'm sorry, and I thought Liam had told you about him." She nervously pats Dax on the head. "He's a foster I took in just before we were asked to come here. I couldn't find anyone to watch—or take him, before we left Georgia. So…I had to bring him along."

Raylene just stares at the dog like it is some wild beast that has wondered into her house. "No, Liam didn't mention him."

"I will find somewhere else for him to stay…I-I'm sorry about all this.'

"You don't have to do that, I would have like to have been warned that I might be licked to death when I returned home." Raylene laughs for the first time since River met her.

"I understand…so…this is Dax…Dax…Raylene." River smiles as she makes the introductions. "I will try to keep him out of your way"

River watches as Raylene turns and heads up the stairs. Taking Dax by the collar she leads him into the guest room. "Bad boy…you can't go giving everybody kisses like that, or I will never find you a home."

River is so caught up in unpacking and setting up everything she will need for surveillance that she doesn't notice the time until her stomach began to rumble, reminding her that she hasn't eaten since early this morning. She has been watching the stairs and front door on the monitor, so she knew Raylene hasn't come downstairs since she arrived home four hours ago. Does she have food up there? Is there a whole other house up there? She run her hands down the front of her slacks, and nervously sets off up the stairs to find where Raylene can be hiding.

All the doors were open except one, so she figures that is where she must be. River gently knocks on the door, and it opens slightly. She sees Raylene sitting on the bed staring at a picture of Nylah that is on the bedside table, tears have streaked her face and the front of her shirt is soaked. "We will find her...I promise." River says softly as she enters the room.

Raylene turns to look at her, "This is all my fault," Raylene couldn't hold back the sobs she feels coming on.

River sits on the bed beside her, "No, it's not, you have nothing to feel guilty about."

"If I hadn't told Kurt, I was leaving...this would have never happened." Raylene covers her face as the sobs come harder. River drapes her arm around this grieving woman's shoulders, just then her phone starts to ring, looking at the screen she notices it is Liam.

"I've got to take this, It's Liam." She walks out into the hallway as she answers the call.

"I thought you were going to help me move my things?" she laughs as she answers. "uh huh...pick up some takeout on your way...I'm starving..."

River sticks her head around the door. "Do you like Chinese?" Raylene stares at her confused, "Food...takeout."

Raylene nods weakly.

Then into the phone, "yes...hurry." She

disconnects the call and goes back to Raylene.

"Why don't you get a shower and freshen up, then come downstairs and have dinner with us."

Raylene doesn't respond but gets up and heads toward her bathroom. River takes that as a yes. As she starts out into the hallway, she stops by Nylah's room. This little girl has everything a girl can dream of. The pink and white lace canopy bed is the most beautiful center piece to the room. The white dresser with its oval mirror captures the entire room like a picture of perfection. She notices the picture of Raylene by her bed, glancing around the room, River wonders why there were no pictures of Kurt in here. She took in the magnificence of the room once more; this is the room she had wanted when she was a little girl. "Nylah, where are you?" River whispers as she closes the door and heads downstairs.

****

River notices that Raylene hasn't said much during dinner. She has eaten even less. After the leftover food has been put away. The three of them moves to the living room to get comfortable and go over what they know at this point. She can tell Raylene still doesn't trust them. It shows in the way she offers very little but asks a lot of questions.

After a while, Raylene sinks back in the oversized sofa and closes her eyes, "So…what you are telling me is that you don't have a clue where Kurt has taken my daughter."

"We need you to tell us all you know about Kurt—

his family/friends—his favorite hangouts—anything you may know to point us in the direction of where to look." Liam pleads with her to open up to them.

River never dreamed that the case they were sent here to investigate would have taken the turn it has. She has pleaded with Liam to be completely honest with Raylene. But he insists that it is too soon. She sits here now wondering if she should override her partner's decision. Liam will no doubt be angry with her. But knowing what Raylene may know about her husband's doings will help them move forward faster.

"What do you know about Kurt's involvement in the drug and prostitution ring?" River can't resist, she must get this woman to talk.

"River—"

"Liam, we are never going to get to the bottom of this unless we stop tip-toeing around the issues." River keeps her eyes on Raylene as she speaks to her partner. She wants to see what Raylene's reaction is going to be.

Raylene's eyes opens as she moves to the edge of the sofa, "What drug and prostitution ring?" she looks to Liam, "What is she talking about?"

River and Liam spend the next hour or more filling her in on how they have been sent to Chicago by request of the Chief of police. They tell her about the suspicions and rumors around town of her husband's involvement in the drug and prostitution ring. Liam tells her about being at the store the night she was stabbed. But that he had no idea she was Kurt's wife, and that Kurt is the one who did this to her. "If I would have known—" Liam let his words trail off.

"If you would have known what?" Raylene urges him to go on.

Liam stands to his feet, running his hand through his hair as he paces around the living room. "I didn't know Kurt had a wife, no one—including the chief knew about you and Nylah—if I would have known—" there is a long pause before he finishes, "Kurt was probably still here when I saw you being put into the ambulance."

"What do you mean by no one knew about me?" Raylene's expression is clear that she is shocked to hear this news.

River reaches across and lays her hand on Raylene's, "We have found no information on a Kurt Sullivan that matches your husband; however, we are still searching."

River listens intently as Raylene fills her in on how she and Kurt had met, she told them about the way he had changed once they were married, and about the way he acted when he had found out she was pregnant, "If I would have known he felt that way about kids, I would have never married him." Raylene can't stop the tears from flowing as she finishes telling the story of the nightmare of a life she has shared with Kurt.

This time it is River who stands and paces the floor, "So—did you ever find out why he was at the hospital?"

Raylene shakes her head no, "I quit asking after a while, I never got anywhere anyway."

River and Liam lock eyes across the room. River

likes the way that she and her partner can communicate without words. "I'm on it." Liam announces as he heads for the door.

He returns a few minutes later with a laptop. After a few clicks he dials a number on his phone. River listens intently as her partner speaks to the person on the phone. *Yes, and that would have been about nine years ago…I'll find out the exact date.* Then the call ends. He shares a look with River that says they need to talk. "Of course, it was a dead end. It seems that is the norm when it comes to finding information on Kurt Sullivan," River notices the way he is looking at her and knows that her partner isn't saying something.

"This would be easier done if we were in Georgia." Liam paces the floor once more as he brainstorms what to do next.

"I am making a trip to Georgia in a few days—I've got to go check on my mom." River stands to join Liam in his pacing. "I could make a trip to Atlanta while there—"

"And investigate the hospital—River, you are awesome!" Liam gives his partner a hug, lifting the tiny woman off her feet. Softly he whispers before letting her go, "I have something I need you to check while there."

River turns toward Raylene who looks perplexed, "We are going to find this scumbag, and get Nylah back home where she belongs." She notices the look of concern that has come over Raylene. River assumes it was the thought of being left alone. "Don't worry, Dax is a wonderful watch dog—I can leave him here with you if you'd like."

Raylene shrugs and nods her head in answer. Dax is laying in the corner of the living room on his oversized dog pillow. At the sound of his name, he stands and walks over to Raylene. "Looks like I have a furry house guest while you are in Georgia." They all laugh as Dax places a wet, sloppy kiss across Raylene's face.

River is happy to see Raylene smile, even if it is a big yellow golden retriever that is the cause. "Looks like Dax agrees also."

Chapter 5

River

Agreeing to meet with Liam before she leaves for Georgia, River sits at the little coffee shop, looking at her watch every two seconds. *Come on, Liam, you know my plane leaves in an hour.* She wonders if she should call him, it's not like him to be late. About the time she reaches for her cellphone, she sees him walk through the door. "It's about time you arrive, I was about to call you," she says to him as he takes a seat across from her.

"I'm sorry, but it's not my fault. An accident had traffic stopped." He motions for the waiter to bring a cup of coffee before he continues. "However, my dear, what I have to tell you about my phone call last night will make the wait worth it."

She leans forward keenly, "Do tell, I knew it was something juicy by the look you gave me."

"Oh, it is beyond juicy—it is downright scandalous!"

"Well! Stop stalling and talk," she hates when he beats around the bush like this. But significantly when she has a flight leaving in less than an hour.

"Nine years ago, there was a Kurt Sullivan who died at that hospital."

"What? No!" Now he really has her attention—forget the plane, she has to hear this. "Do you think our Kurt is somehow related to that Kurt Sullivan?"

"I'd find it odd that he was there around the same time if he wasn't related in some way." He takes a sip of his coffee before going on, "but, my precious dove, you are going to find out for us. When you arrive go straight to the hospital and see what you can dig up, there may be someone working there at the time that may know something, so talk to everyone you can. Then go to the police station and see what they have on this Kurt Sullivan—it appears he was in an automobile accident, so I'm sure there are records of that on file, and—"

"You do realize I am taking a few days off to visit with my mom?" she laughs as she throws a sugar pack across the table. "But I know the drill—talk to everyone at the hospital—investigate everyone and every file at PD—check all the newspapers—I got it." She stands and pushes the chair under the table as she throws a twenty in front of him, "but-darlin' dearest, I have a plane to catch, or I won't be going to Georgia today."

"I'll email you the rest," he shouts to her back as she rushes out the door.

****

The plane had seemed to take forever to get to Atlanta. River had vowed to herself that she would spend at least two days visiting with her mom before jumping into the case. But after spending a sleepless night going over the details that Liam had sent her, she is eager to get started digging deeper into the drama. This case is better than any dramatic scene she has ever watch on the television.

After printing off all the information in the email, she shoves everything into her bag and heads for the door. Having already explained to her mom that she has some things to do today, she doesn't bother waking her now to tell her she is leaving. The hospital is her first stop, and in Atlanta traffic, it takes her a while to get there.

Once there, a receptionist points her to the RN Liam had spoken with on the phone. The two decide to have this conversation over lunch in the cafeteria. River is getting tired of the usual small talk the RN is pursuing. "I'm sorry to change the subject, but I must get back to my mom and I still have a few other stops to make." Finally, she decides on being direct, "Tell me what you know about the Kurt Sullivan that was admitted here nine years ago."

"All I really know is that he was sent here because of the seriousness of his injuries. He was involved in a single-car accident, and he—died from those injuries."

"What about family? Do you recall any family that may have visited?"

"Actually, yes—there was a daughter that stayed by his side the entire time. But what I find strange is—" She pushes her lunch aside and is absently fidgeting with her ring, "—there was a son also, he was here just like the daughter; but he never would enter his dad's room. He would stop by and stand in the door for a few seconds, then go come back down here or in the smoker's pavilion."

"Do you happen to know the daughter or son's name?"

"Yes, I remember both well. Brenda and Trevor. I only know this because she used to scream at him and he at her."

"About what?"

"From what I gathered, it was Trevor who was driving the car, and apparently, he had been drinking prior to offering to drive his parents; no one knew about his drinking, so they let him drive." The RN shrugs her shoulders, "I don't know if it's true or not, but that's what Brenda was yelling at her brother."

"Would you happen to have an address on file for the family?"

"Yes, I have all that information in this packet I put together for you." She takes a manilla folder from her over-sized lunch bag, handing it to River she adds, "I am not supposed to release this information, but Detective

Geoffrey explained to me about the little girl missing, if this can help find her, I'm willing to break the rules."

"What you are doing will be kept confidential. We will never tell anyone you gave this information to us; I promise." River pushes back her chair as she stands, "If you think of anything else that might be helpful, please call me." She hands her business card to the nurse and walks away.

God is really smiling down on her today. Getting a police officer to talk about a case without a court order is almost impossible. Yet today, she found one willing to spill all about the Sullivan case. "So, you're telling me that Trevor Sullivan disappeared just before his dad passed away and has never been found since."

"That's correct; we have searched all of Georgia and he seems to have just vanished off the face of the earth." Lieutenant Mike Blakely shakes his head in defeat, "His sister hasn't seen or heard from him either. She says it's for the best, because he's dead to her anyway—you know how family feuds go."

"Do you think the sister would speak with me if I went out to ask her a few questions?"

"I really can't say. She is pretty bitter against her brother."

"I think it would be worth a try; would you happen to know where I can find her?"

"She's living in her parents old house, she moved in there after their death—I reckon she's trying to tend to the farm and keep it going."

River nods, "I see—so—what kind of farm do they have?"

"Cattle—I don't know how Sullivan kept that place going with him being a cop and all, but somehow he managed." He gives a low chuckle, "and with the trouble that boy was always getting into—" he lets his words trail off as he shakes his head.

"The son has priors?"

"Oh, yeah—a list about a mile long; it's public record if you'd like to take a look."

"Could I? I would love to," she hopes she doesn't seem too eager.

He leads her to a room in the back; she sees rolls upon rolls of file boxes. The musky smell of the room is almost more than her stomach can take. They pass the boxes to the back of the room, where there is a single roll of tall file cabinets along the entire wall. He leads her to the one marked with a big *S,* then opens the drawer that reads *Sullivan, Trevor.*

"He has so many priors that he has his own drawer." He chuckles again before adding, "I'll leave you to it—good luck."

"Thanks" It would take days for her to sort through all this. She runs her finger over the tabs, reading each folder. 'Drunk driving,' 'disorderly conduct,' 'discharging a firearm,' 'domestic violence.' This last one intrigues her the most; removing it from the cabinet, she walks over to a table nearby and starts to read over each page. *What? I can't believe what I am reading.* Taking a notebook from her bag, she copies the information; *I can't wait to tell Liam about this—wow, just wow!* She puts the folder back in its place and turns to find her way out.

River thanks the Lieutenant for his time and heads out to her car. Deciding this is enough searching for one day, she opts to go home and examine the information she has already before pursuing the sister. But unfortunately, Liam is going to have to wait also. She wants to hear the sister out before sharing anything with him.

****

Driving through the countryside of Georgia makes River want to reconsider her decision to move to the city. Because as she pulls onto the long driveway that leads to Brenda Sullivan, she can understand why the choice was made to keep the family farm. The fenced fields on each side of the drive are serenely breathtaking. As she pulls up to the house, a woman dressed in battered jeans and a plaid, button-down shirt over a soiled t-shirt is walking toward the house from the nearby barn.

River puts the car in park and exits the vehicle. She waves to the woman who is now walking in her direction. "Hello, I'm looking for Brenda Sullivan." She doesn't notice that she forgot to introduce herself. If Raylene's husband were a female, this is precisely what he would look like. They are almost identical.

"Who wants to know?"

"I'm sorry, I'm Detective River Donaldson—"

"I need you to leave right now please."

"I want to ask you some questions about your brother. We hav—"

"Goodbye, Detective." She turns to walk away.

"Miss Sullivan, please—"

"I don't have a brother—so leave now."

"He may have tried to kill someone in Chicago, and he is now on the run with a little four-year-old girl." River rushes the words to stop her, and it works.

Brenda slowly turns around but remains silent.

"Please, answer a few questions for me." River hopes her pleading will break through the anger this woman holds against her brother.

"Chicago. Is that where he's been hiding?"

"We don't know. I have some pictures of the man we are looking for, if you don't mind take a look and tell us if he is your brother." River reaches in the car for the picture of Kurt and holds it out to the woman.

Brenda walks closer and takes it from her. Tears spring to her eyes as she stares at the picture in her hand. "It's him," she whispers, "Come in and we'll talk." She hands the image back to River and turns to walk towards the house.

They spend the better part of an hour talking about Raylene and Nylah. Then, knowing she has a long drive back into Atlanta, she knew she had to move the conversation along. "Tell me about his first wife."

Brenda jerks her head up, "What do you want to know about her?"

"I know about the domestic violence charges against your brother."

"He blamed her for their daughter's death; and—"

"They had a daughter?" River was shocked to hear this news; no one at the police department mentioned anything about a daughter.

"Yes, she was two when she—" she let her words trail off, unable to say the word. "Beth Ann had fell asleep while watching tv with her; the front door was open and she wondered outside and—she didn't know not to go near the road, and—" Brenda begins to sob uncontrollably.

"You can stop," River whispers as she takes the woman's hand in hers, "I am smart enough to figure out the rest; What happened to Beth Ann?"

"Two days before the anniversary of that tragic day, Trevor had too much to drink, and he almost killed her." She stopped and took a deep breath before continuing. "In a way I guess he did. The injuries were so bad—she is paralyzed for life."

"How did he not get sent down the road for that."

"He did. After serving two years of a ten-year sentence, they let him out on parole; he was still on probation when he killed my parents."

"That's why he ran." River stated more to herself than to Brenda, "He would have never seen the light of day with all those charges hanging over him, so—he ran."

Everything was starting to come together, like the pieces of a zig-saw puzzle. River couldn't wait to call Liam and tell him all she had uncovered on this dirtbag. After making plans to set up a time for the two of them to visit with Beth Ann, she gathers her notes and heads back to her mom's house.

River was elated that she had unearthed so much on Kurt, or at least the man they thought to be Kurt. She now knew that Raylene has been sharing a life with a monster named Trevor. However, the fact that monster has Nylah was an unsettling thought to her; she has all this information but still not a clue where he is hiding. And hiding seems to be something he is very good at. After all, he's managed to stay hidden for nine years from his family.

Upon arriving back at the house, she rushes upstairs to email Liam. 'Call me asap—you're not going to believe what I have to tell you.'
■■■

Chapter 6
Raylene

Raylene stretches as she comes awake; suddenly, there is a loud thud by the bed. She throws the covers back and peers over the edge, "Sorry, Dax, I forgot about you." The dog gives a low snort and moves toward the window; walking in a slow circle, he plops down, cutting his sad eyes towards her as if to say, *was that necessary?* Raylene rises from the bed and starts towards the bathroom, "I never gave you permission to sleep on the bed anyway, don't be having an attitude with me when it's your fault."

Having a dog around is going to take some getting used to. Kurt hates animals about as much as he seems to dislike people. She isn't sure he likes anyone as much as he enjoys himself. Everything has to be the way he wants it, no questions, no exceptions. She had wanted to paint the bathroom yellow, and he wanted blue…blue is what they got. She had desired the maroon-colored curtains, with the lacy ruffles in the living room; he had wanted dark brown with no ruffles…their living room still sports those ugly curtains. Even when it comes to food, if she wants chicken, he orders steak.

She barely finishes getting dressed when the doorbell echoes through the house. Liam seems to always be on time. Can't he ever be a few minutes late? Dax is right on her heels as she starts down the stairs. "Oh, so you perk up when you know someone is here. Do you not enjoy my company?" the dog rushes past her and sniffs at the door. Smiling down at the dog, excitingly awaiting her to reveal who is waiting on the other side, she opens the door. Her smile fades when she realizes Liam is not alone.

"Why is he here?" she asks Liam while looking skeptically at Ronny standing just behind him. "You know I asked that no cops be involved; I only agreed on you and River."

"You do remember that Ronny is the reason River and I are here?" Liam shoves his hand in his front pockets; Raylene notices that he does that when he's nervous.

Ronny walks up beside Liam, "I want to find Kurt and that little girl as bad as you do; please, let's work together on this."

Raylene looks back and forth between the two, blowing out a loud sigh; she opens the door wide to allow the two to enter, "I guess I can hear what you have to say; come in." She says as she closes the door behind them. "Have a seat, please." She waves towards the sofa as she takes the chair across from them. Ronny is Kurt's boss; that alone is a reason for her not to trust him, but she will hear what he has to say, then send him on his way.

"I'm waiting." She states as she sits back in the chair and folds her arms across her chest.

Ronny moves to the edge of the sofa, "Can you tell me about your husband before you met him? Where did he live, where is his family, how did you meet? Those sort of things…" he trails off.

"I've already told Detective Liam and River everything I know. Kurt is a private person; he doesn't speak of his family, and it angers him when I ask about them. That's all I have to tell you about my husband." She inhales and slowly exhales before finishing, "To say the least…I don't know very much about my husband. Honestly, I don't think I know him at all."

Ronny looks towards Liam and whispers softly, "Do you want to tell her or me?"

Liam nods for him to continue.

"I don't know how to say this, so I'm just going to give it to you straight," he pauses and glances back to Liam, then sits back as he continues. "Your husband isn't who you think he is." He let Raylene take that in before he starts again. "We have been digging to find information on him for a while now; Kurt Daniel Sullivan is dead; he died nine years ago in an automobile accident. Liam tells me that the two of you met at Emory Hospital in Atlanta, Georgia, going on nine years ago; is that correct?"

Raylene only nods in response; she can't find her voice to speak. If he's not Kurt Sullivan, then who is he? And why is he lying about who he is?

"We think he may be the person that was driving the car when Mr. Sullivan was injured and later died from those injuries." Ronny rubs his hands over his face, "Why he would take the name of the person—" he takes a minute to process his thoughts, "We think his name is Trevor Michael Sullivan…Kurt's son."

Raylene holds up her palm to stop him, "How did you come to this conclusion?"

"They were returning from a trip. Both parents were in the vehicle; Trevor fell asleep at the wheel, left the roadway, and struck a tree. His mother died at the scene. Mr. Sullivan never regained consciousness, Trevor was

arrested for DUI, but was released to be with his father—
he disappeared when his father passed."

Liam leans forward, "We don't know for sure if he
is the missing son, we only know that Trevor disappeared
and has never been found since that day. He would have
been at the hospital during the time you and your family
was there."

Raylene is confused, not knowing what to say. "He
left for Chicago before my father passed away, said it was
an emergency he had to get back."

"See, that's the kicker." Ronny began, "Kurt was
offered a job in Chicago and planned to move here within
a month of the accident. I called to ask if he could come
earlier; his son took the call." Ronny continues to tell how
he speculates that Trevor used that to escape prosecution.
"We think he knew his father was going to die and took
the job under his dad's name—and for nine years he has
gotten away with it."

Raylene shakes her head, "But—that doesn't
explain everything—"

"The drug and prostitution ring?" Liam asks as he
nudges Ronny.

Knowing what the Detective was urging he
scratches his head; "Yeah, we now know he wasn't
involved in any of that. We've observed him a few times
having secret meetings with a—" he searches for the right
word to describe the people, "—nefarious looking
couple."

"We have discovered that those people are not as
nefarious as we thought." Liam interjects. "But they're

not telling us why they were privately meeting with Kurt, only that he is a nice person who helps them."

"Helps them how?" Nothing gets past her. She wants all the details.

Ronny is the one to answer, "We observed him giving them money, and later they would give him a package. Then, like clockwork, they would meet, mostly on holidays. We found Trevor's parents' graves in Georgia; someone keeps fresh flowers and letters on their tombstone. We assume that it is this couple who has been doing so."

Raylene's mind is reeling. None of this makes sense to her. If Kurt is Trevor and pretending to be his dead father, what does this mean to her and Nylah? Then there is the question that plagues her the most, "If what you are telling me is true, how has this not been discovered by now?" She stands to pace the room, "It's been nine years—Nine. Years."

Liam nods for Ronny to answer.

"Georgia and Chicago are far apart, for one. Up until recently, we didn't have a reason to investigate his past—I thought Kurt was the one who showed up to work with the PD." Ronny stood and walked towards Raylene, "Believe it or not, things like this happen all the time."

"Why did he keep me a secret? What does this all mean for the two of us?" She is hoping the Chief had answers for her. God knows she needs them.

"You are not legally married." Ronny shrugs his shoulders, "Thus, the private ceremony. My theory is he could not marry you because this would have revealed his secret long ago."

"You married a dead man. Thus, being discovered more quickly; so, he kept you secret." Liam injects. "And we have found out that no birth certificate was ever file for Nylah."

She suddenly feels dizzy. Her entire life for the past nine years has been a lie. "I need time to process all of this information," she walks to the door to see the men out, "Could you please go now?"

Liam stops in the doorway, "As you know, River is in Georgia; hopeful she will have some concrete answers for us soon. I'll contact you as soon as she confirms the information, we shared with you tonight."

As she closes the door behind them, she stands with her back to the door. Her gaze stops on a picture above the sofa. It is of the two of them on the day they were married out in the gazebo in the front yard. Taking in the way he holds her, the way he lovingly stares into her eyes. *Who are you, and why did you bring me into this?* And sweet Nylah, so young and so innocent.

She needs to lie down; so, she makes her way up the stairs. Instead of going to her room, she slowly opens Nylah's door, taking in the beautiful space she has made for her daughter. This room holds everything a little girl could dream of. She walks around the room touching all the dolls, and rocking horse, clothes, and shoes. Then finally, picking up the blanket that is laying on the foot of the bed, she holds it to her face and inhales the scent of her little girl. Curling up on the tiny twin bed, she falls asleep with the blanket held tightly in her arms.

****

Raylene glances at the clock on the kitchen wall as she starts towards the front door, where Dax is running in circles and barking like a dog gone mad. "Okay, buddy, I'll let you out. But do not leave the yard and come straight back." She feels weird talking to a dog as if it is human. It must be a typical occurrence; she sees people at the park doing it all the time. "I don't know why you can't use the doggie pad I put out for you; do you know what time it is?" She removes the safety chain and unlocks the door, "It is after eleven o'clock at night—hurry back."

Dax darts out the door as soon as she opens it and springs across the yard, barking and growling as he rounds the hedge bushes out onto the sidewalk. "Dax!" she screams as she runs after the dog. Not as agile as a canine, she decides to run down the driveway instead of across the front lawn. Rounding the corner onto the sidewalk; she doesn't see the man standing there, chest to chest, they both tumble to the ground.

"I am so sorry." Raylene scrambles to get back on her feet, "I-I didn't see you there. I-I'm trying to catch m-my dog." Fear courses through her as she realizes this could have been Kurt. But who is he, and why is he at the end of her driveway?

"I-It's okay, m-ma'am," the man dusts off his black shirt and jeans as he looks her over, "ar-are, you o-okay?"

"I'm fine. I just skinned my elbow." She holds up her arm for him to see. Dax is at the man's feet, bouncing and barking, pouncing on the ground with the hairs on his neck and back raised. "Dax, come, boy," the dog obeys and comes to stand at her side. He continues to give a low growl as he peers up at this strange man.

"Are you hurt?" she says to the man, "You took the brunt of the fall."

"I just need to wash my hands; do you mind if I come inside to—you know?" he wrings his hands in a washing motion. "M-My name is Wyatt, by the way."

Raylene looks at the house, then back to the man, unsure what to do; his spikey orange hair, all-black attire, with chains looping from his jean pockets, along with the tattoo's covering his arms and several on his face, gives him a gang member appearance.

"It will only take a minute; and it would be nice to warm up a bit."

"I-I think it will be alright," she takes Dax by the collar and heads toward the house.

Once in the house, the dog watches Wyatt like a hawk as Raylene leads him to the half bath near the kitchen. "How long have you had the dog?" he is trying to make small talk as he exits the tiny bathroom.

"He belongs to a friend. I'm just dog-sitting," she answers a bit confused as she watches him walk to the sofa and have a seat. She doesn't want him in her house and wishes that he would leave.

"Thanks a lot, Raylene, for letting me come in; it feels nice and toasty in here."

The hair on her arms raises at the sound of her name. *How does he know my name? I never introduced myself.* "Would you like some coffee? It will help warm you faster." In times like this, she is proud of her quick wit in destressing moments.

"That would be nice, if it's not too much trouble."

"Not at all," she replies as she heads into the kitchen. Once out of sight, she removes her cellphone from her pocket. Praying that Liam was still awake she texts him, '911'. Almost immediately, her phone rings. "Okay, get as soon as you can," then she ends the call. Liam had asked if everything was alright; she prays he is bright enough to know she needs him here now. Taking the cup of coffee from the Keurig, she heads back to the living room.

"Looks like your mom will be late tomorrow," she says to Dax as she enters the room. Not knowing if Wyatt has heard the exchange, she felt using the dog is a good coverup. As she hands the hot coffee to him, she realizes she hasn't asked if he wants cream and sugar. He took a sip as soon as he receives it. *If he doesn't ask for it, I'm not offering it.*

"Do you stay here alone?" Wyatt asks as he looks around the room and up the stairs, "This seems like a large house for one person."

She nervously rubs her palms on her thighs; as she speaks, she glances towards the door, "No, I have a—," *a what? Think quickly, Raylene.* "—a roommate that has been staying with me lately."

"Oh, I see," he sits the cup on the coffee table. "I'm sorry if all the commotion has awakened them," he glances once again towards the stairs.

"No, no. He is not here now." *Stupid—stupid Raylene, now he knows you're alone in the house;* she scolds herself for not thinking before she spoke.

"He?" Wyatt seems overly interested in her statement.

"Well, they, actually. She's out of town this week." *Liam, where are you?* As soon as this thought enters her mind, she hears the car come up the driveway. "Sounds like he's here now." Walking to the door, she sighs with relief.

Liam is already at the door by the time she opens it. "I was wondering if you were coming home tonight," giving a wink as she turns to lead him into the room. "This is Wy—"

"Wyatt Kapers?" he storms towards the man, "What are you doing here?"

"I-I just c-came in to w-wash my hands and warm up a little," Wyatt begins nervously, "I-I'm just leaving."

Liam shoves him back down on the sofa, "You're not going anywhere. Tell me where he is?"

"Will someone tell me what is going on?" Raylene looks from one man to the other.

Liam is the one who speaks, "This is the man we told you about earlier this morning—the couple, his wife's name is Sarah." Then, looking down at Wyatt, he continues, "Where is she? We know that she is never too far away from you."

No one hears the door as it opens, "I'm r-right here," Raylene looks the girl over. She now understands why the police department thought Kurt was involved in a drug and prostitution ring. But, of course, hanging around people like this would give someone that idea.

Sarah is wearing a black mini skirt, a red single-shoulder shirt with holes in various places, with a black halter top underneath it. Her hair boasts the same bright orange as her husband's, only purple streaks peeking through it. "W-we really don't know where Mr. Sullivan is." She speaks so softly; if one didn't listen closely, you wouldn't know she spoke at all.

"You told me and the chief that you didn't know him, why?" Raylene has never seen Liam's face so red, "A little girl's life is at stake—and you lied about being involved with him."

"You don't understand," Wyatt begins before being cut off by Liam.

"Then help me understand—start talking."

"H-his family don't like him none." Sarah offered.

"Sarah, we have done nothing wrong, you don't got to tell these people anything."

Raylene saunters towards Sarah, "He may have killed his parents, he tried to kill me; now he has my little girl. If you know anything that can help us, please, I'm begging you—tell us." She feels the tears as they burn down her face. *Please, God, let them talk if they know where this monster has my baby.*

Wyatt takes his wife by the arm and leads her towards the door, "I was walking by, and this woman mows me over trying to get her dog, I asked to come in and wash up, and get warm. That is all that happened. Pick on someone else please."

"Oh, now I'm 'this lady'." Raylene storms towards the couple, "Just a little while ago you called me by my name—how do you know what my name is?"

"Y-you told me,"

"No, I didn't."

"Leave us alone, you—you people are crazy. Me and Sarah have done nothing, so-so, leave us alone," he slams the door behind them.

"Liam, go stop them," she yells at him as he tries to pull her in his arms to calm her.

"Raylene, please. We have nothing to keep them here on." He leads her to the sofa and sits her there, "In time, they will have to speak up; I promise we will find Nylah."

Collapsing in his embrace, she finally let go of the floodgate she has been holding in since this all began. Liam holds her tightly as her body heaves with sobs. "I-I pray every night, that God will bring her back to me." She pushes away and swipes at the tears dripping from her chin. "Alive and well." Through renewed sobs, she continues, "Liam, I cannot go on without her, for four years, she has been what has kept me going. She's my life, my everything."

"I know, and I'll find her—if it's the last thing I do." Liam leans back on the sofa, never letting her go as she weeps in his arm.

Raylene clings tightly to the safety of Liam's arm. Even after the sobbing stops, she remains in his embrace as she drifts off to sleep.

∎∎∎∎∎∎∎∎∎∎∎∎∎∎∎∎∎∎∎∎∎∎∎∎∎∎∎∎∎∎∎∎∎∎∎∎∎∎∎

Chapter 7
Liam

Waking up with Raylene cuddled up close beside him would be much better under different circumstances. Liam doesn't know what it is about this woman that makes him want to help her so much. He has worked tons of cases throughout his career but never has he felt such a connection as the one he has with Raylene. Holding on to her last night as she cried herself to sleep broke his heart into a million pieces. As he stands over the sofa watching her sleep, he hates to wake her. But she's going to want to hear about the phone conversation he just had with River.

"Why are you standing there staring at me?" Raylene whispers without opening her eyes.

"I-I'm stalling about waking you, you look so peaceful and rested." He smiles down at her.

"So, you just stand there and stare at me?" she returns his smile as she pushes up to a sitting position.

"I am anxious to share what River had to say on the phone just now."

Her eyes went wide with anticipation. "Tell me— did she find him? What did she find out about the other stuff? Is he—"

"Whoa, one thing at a time." Liam runs his hands through his hair and then shoves them into his pockets before continuing. "She found his sister and—"

"He has a sister? Wow, I have a sister-in-law." She shrugs smugly, taking in the news, "Is he Kurt or is he Trevor?"

"It is the way we suspected. He is Trevor."

Liam spent the next hour filling her in on everything River uncovered about her husband. He pauses ever so often to give her time to absorb each new blow. Giving her time to know the real man she married. He watches as she stands and paces the living room. How could any man want to hurt this woman? She's not beautiful in the traditional sense; her dark hair isn't long and flowing but kept cropped in a short back with longer sides that frame her face in just the perfect way. Her hazel eyes turning a different color with the changes in lighting. Right now, they look green, which seems to be the color that suits her best. Her full mouth is drawn in a slight pucker; apparently, this is the way she holds her mouth when in deep thought, he has noticed that about her over the last few days. If only they could have met at another time, back before Kurt, back before all this craziness—*what? Where were you going with that thought, ole boy?*

"Liam why does God hate me?" she says, bringing him out of his thoughts.

"What makes you think that He hates you?"

"Where do I start?" she remarks as she pushes back on the sofa, pulling her knees into her chest, "He allowed me to fall in love with a monster of a man, that man has made my life—and my daughter's—a living hell."

Liam just sat quietly, listening intently to the words that seemed to spill from her heart.

"Did I ever tell you that I had to hire a nanny to make sure Kurt never saw her?"

He nodded.

"He told me that he never gave me permission to have a kid—like she was some animal I brought home off the street." She rises from the sofa and walks over to stare out the window, "As she got older, he made remarks like, *you need to clean up better after that kid or I want it out of here. or,* when she could be heard crying at night he'd say, *is there not somewhere else you can put that thing? Have you ever thought about the basement?"*

"How could someone be so cold towards a child?" Liam found himself wanting to wrap her in his arms and make all the hurt go away. It took a lot of restraint to remain within professional limits with this woman. Especially watching her wipe at the tears streaming down her face.

Raylene doesn't respond; she keeps her eyes trained on whatever she is focusing on outside. After a while, she continues with her story. "Now, God has let that monster take my daughter. But not without trying to kill me first—If God cared about me, would He allow all these things to happen?" she turns to face him as if he—Liam—held all the answers.

"All I can tell you is—" not knowing what to say but wanting to say the right thing, he pauses to gather his thoughts, "Raylene, God doesn't hate you. Bad things happen in life all the time, and most of the time to good people—like you." He walks over to where she is standing, "We all go through things that we don't understand. Those things can make us feel like God is nowhere around—but He is. If nothing bad ever happened, we wouldn't know that He can fix it. This is not happening *to* you—it's happening *for* you. God will bring your daughter back, and when He does—things will be better than they were before."

"I hope you're right." She turns back to the window, "Even though I can't tell if He is listening or not—I pray every day that He will keep Nylah safe and bring her home to me."

Liam was relieved she hadn't asked how he knew all these things. This was a lesson he was still learning. Losing his wife shortly after they married, Liam had decided to put work above everything in his life. Work seemed to be what got him through those first few weeks after Lisa's death. Yet, the thought of that day still puts a pain in his heart. They had just arrived back home from their honeymoon. Lisa had wanted to run out to the store to pick up some things they needed; he had let her go, not knowing that would be the last time he saw her alive. Not knowing that at that very moment, some fool had decided to drive drunk and run the red light she was about to drive under; not knowing that he would strike his wife's car at a speed so fast that it would split her car almost in half— taking his wife's life instantly. In the ten years since her death, he had never thought about dating again. No one ever interested him—until now.

"Lisa, I'm sorry I had to be the one to tell you all this," he reaches out and takes her hand, "I just wish we could have found out more about his whereabouts."

Raylene didn't answer just stared at him blankly.

"What? Why are you looking at me like that?"

"You've been quiet for a long time while I was mulling over the information you gave me," she said as she retrieved the hand he was holding, "What were you thinking about?"

He shook his head, "Just wishing I had more to go on—why?"

"Who is Lisa?"

"Wha—"

"You called me Lisa." She gave him a slight smile.

"Oh, I didn't realize—She was my wife, I was just thinking about her and before you ask—she was killed about ten years ago in an accident."

"Oh, okay. I'm sorry to hear that." The way Raylene looks at him makes him nervous. "I've also noticed the way you look at me and you do realize I'm married right?"

"Raylene, I'm sorry if I—I'm sorry." He run his hands down his jeans, "I think I'm going to go and let you absorb all this—information." He needed to get out of here fast.

"I'll call if I have any questions." She said as she walks him to the door.

"And I'll call if I find out anything more." He never looks back as he walks to his car. He felt like such a fool right now—an unprofessional fool.

****

He slams the laptop closed and pushes it back to clear up his desk. Liam takes the stack of papers that River had sent to him and starts to spread them over the space in front of him; this case had taken a turn that he hadn't expected. Who would have known that Kurt was Trevor and above all, he was a wanted man for being responsible for his parents' death? But then, to find out that he has a wife and a child that died. All this was almost too much for him to comprehend; he could only imagine how Raylene must feel.

Now, according to River's email, she needs him in Georgia. How can he leave her now? How can he dump something like this on her and then just leave her? He would like to think that this trip wouldn't take long, but it was hard to tell with things like this. Ronny will be around if Trevor should show up while he was away. But somehow leaving her just does not feel right.

As he reads over the papers in front of him, he can't figure out how this man has outsmarted the cops all these years. He has gotten away with being a cop all this time. For all Liam knows, he could be hiding right under their noses, and they just haven't discovered him yet. *He could know every move we're making—laughing at us for not being able to find him.*

He pushes back in his chair and reaches for his phone. *Please let her answer.* He pleads as he listens to the ringing on the other end, "Raylene, Hi, it's Liam." He began as she answers the phone, "I need to come by and talk with you—is now a good time?" he prays she doesn't feel uncomfortable with the way he acted earlier. "You're at the state park with Dax? —okay—I can come there if you don't mind me intruding—all right, see you in a few minutes."

He pushes the chair back and stands to gather all the paperwork and stuff them in his briefcase. All he can do now is pray that she will be safe until he returns. And pray even harder that she doesn't feel like they are abandoning her.

■■

Chapter 8
Raylene

Raylene sits and stares at the phone in her hand long after she ended the call with Liam. Why couldn't she have met this man a lifetime ago? Before Kurt—or Trevor—whoever he is. Liam is a man she could love;

he's charming in an awkward kind of way. Even though she would never tell him, it was as if God had sent her an angel in the middle of all the madness. Last night reminded her of how long it has been since she had been in a man's embrace. Granted, it would have been better under different circumstances.

She takes her eyes off the phone and looks around the park. This bench seems to have been placed in the perfect location. Every angle of the park was visible from here. Why hasn't she ever brought Nylah here? The play area is state of the art, with swings and monkey bars, and slides of all shapes and sizes. She would love the titter-totters; they are miniature animals of all sorts; the unicorn would probably be her favorite. Raylene's eyes dim as tears flood them with the thought of her daughter. What she wouldn't give to have her back safe where she belongs.

Suddenly she remembers she came here with Dax. Where is he? Across the park at the far side, she spots a man sitting on a picnic table, Dax is there with him. The man seems to be staring right at her. *Is that Kurt?* Raylene trembles as she slowly stands. *That looks like Kurt.* She watches as the man steps down off the table, never taking his eyes from her direction. He reaches inside his blazer; she knows that Kurt keeps his gun holstered there. Her heart races, and her palms grow sweaty as she slowly moves around the bench, picking up her pace as she heads for the forest line at the edge of the park. She never looks back as she darts in and out around the trees.

Are those footsteps she hears behind her? Has he followed her? She doesn't know if the sound she hears is the crunching of leaves underneath someone's feet or if it is the blood that is rushing through her body; she just keeps running faster and faster through the trees. She finally stops to catch her breath behind a big Oaktree. She tries hard to slow her breathing. There's that crunching sound again; he is following her! She looks around for something to use for protection. Her foot bumps against a softball-sized rock, she slowly slides down the tree to pick it up. She grips it tightly with both her shaking hands and raises it above her head.

She can hardly steady herself as she hears the footsteps getting closer; she looks to her right side and spots a shadow approaching. Darting her eyes back and forth, not knowing which side of this enormous tree he will appear. Then suddenly…

"Raylene—"

The sound is on her left. Turning quickly, seeing only the figure of a man, she brings the rock down with all the force she can muster. As she drops the rock, she darts away from the tree, glancing back as the figure collapses to the ground. She stops in her tracks as she looks at the man lying there, "Liam?" she gasped.

She rushes to his aid, "I am sorry—Kurt was there—he had a gun—"

"Raylene—"

"He was staring at me—he reached for his gun and—"

"Raylene!" Liam gropes for her out reached hand, "Help me up." Once he was on his feet, he rubs his forehead, feeling a goose egg already forming, he looks at his hand, "At least there's no blood," he says absently.

Raylene reaches up and lightly strokes the lump that is already turning a bluish-black, "I really am sorry. I thought you were Kurt."

"Help me back to the park so I can sit for a moment." He leans into her as she helps him steady himself for the walk back.

She settled him at a picnic table and started scanning the park, "We need ice." Spotting a soda machine near the bathrooms she searches her pockets for some change, "Do you have a quarter? I am one short."

"Why do you need a quarter?"

"To buy a soda." She takes the quarter he offers her and runs to the machine.

"You want a soda? Now?" he yells after her.

She returns with the cold soda and Dax trotting beside her, wagging his tail happily. She plops the can on the knot forming on his head, "Here—hold this on there for a minute. Look who I found while I was gone," she nods towards the dog, "What a good watch dog he was." She laughs.

"Wow, you really know how to improvise, don't you?" Liam holds the cold soda to his head with one hand and playfully scratches Dax's head with the other.

"It's not ice—but it's cold." She shrugs as she sits down beside him. "I think we need to get you to the hospital and have that looked at."

"I'll be fine, I have a plane to catch—so there's no time for that."

"You're leaving?"

"Yes, that's what I was coming to tell you," He lowers the can and pops the top, taking a big gulp before continuing, "River needs me in Georgia—it'll only be for few days—a week at the most."

"I'm not trying to change the subject, but I feel like such a fool right now." She says as she stares off in the distance. "See the guy with the two boys over there?" she nods her head in the direction of a man with what appears to be twin toddlers. "That's the guy I thought was Kurt. I just panicked and ran." She covers her face with her hands and giggles softly.

"I'm glad you have the ability to laugh at yourself in times like this—you are amusing,"

"Amusing how?"

"You laugh at your calamities, and use cold soda for a compress—what other tricks do you have up your sleeve?"

"I'm a pretty good aim with a rock." She laughs as she touches the knot on his forehead.

"Ouch! You love torching me, don't you?"

"Now back to your trip. When will you be leaving?"

"My flight leaves in about three hours."

"Can I come along? Mom lives in Georgia; I've been planning on getting away from here for a while and visit with her."

He looks at her in amazement, "There you go again with your brilliant ideas—I think it would do you good to get out of here—for a little bit anyway."

"Well, if we're going—I need to pack and—wait—what about the house—what if Kurt comes back there?"

"Ronny will be keeping an eye on things here."

"You had asked him to babysit me?" Dax rubs against her leg, "Oh, wait! What about Dax? We can't leave him here alone."

"Babysit—no! I only asked if he would—"

Raylene laughed, "I'm kidding—chill."

"I'll ask Ronny to keep an eye on Dax until we get back."

"Sounds like a plan—let's get moving then—before you make us miss our flight.

"Improvisational, risible, and—bossy." Liam chuckled as she jabs his ribs. "Let's go to Georgia." He laughs.

Once arriving in Georgia, Raylene was surprised to find that Liam had called ahead to have a rental car waiting there for her also. Seeing they both needed to go in different directions, two would be better than one. As she turns the Toyota Corolla onto her mom's driveway, she suddenly grows anxious. She has not seen her mother in person for almost nine years. The closest she has come is facetiming her on social media. Her heart aches at knowing she has never got to hug and kiss her beautiful granddaughter and wishes so badly that Nylah could be making this trip with her. Soon, she thinks—God, I pray it's soon—my daughter will be back in my arms.

As she nears the house, childhood memories wash over her filling her with nostalgia. Oh, how she missed her dad. Growing up, she was always a daddy's girl. Seeing the tractor parked over to the side of the yard, right where he last left it, brought back memories of hot southern summer days she spent on there with him plowing the fields. Now, it was just a rusted heap of metal, its paint flaked and peeling. Parked not too far from it was his 1980s Ford F150 pickup. That, too, brought back many memories of the two of them going fishing and sitting on the tailgate, waiting for the fish to bite. At the same time, her dad recited stories from the Bible to her, or they sit there singing his favorite hymns, mostly Amazing Grace, which was the one he sang the most.

Seeing her mom open the old screen door, with her hand at her brow line, shielding the sun to see who was approaching, brought her back to the present. She hadn't called ahead to tell her mom she was coming; the element of surprise was always the best choice. The moment of recognition registers on her mom's face. Raylene giggles as the frail, gray hair woman starts to run toward the car before she has a chance to come to a complete stop.

"Raylene! Oh, my goodness, God has finally answered my prayers and brought my baby home!" Ruth Smith opens the door and practically pulls her from the vehicle.

Raylene giggles, "Woah, let me exit on my own." Her mom takes her in a bear hug as soon as she is out. "Mom, I can't breathe," she laughs.

"I can't help it! It seems like forever since I was able to coddle you." The aging woman places her hands on Raylene's shoulders and straightens her arms, "Let me look at you—oh, you are a sight for sore eyes—as beautiful as ever." Looping her arm around her daughter's elbow, she leads her towards the house, "but, you look exhausted. Let's get you inside and put some food in you—I will tidy up your room while you eat; you look like you could use a nap, then we will talk and catch up on things—how's that sound."

"Honestly—that sounds like an awesome plan. I will not argue with you." She smiles as they walk through the door, "Mm, something smells delicious in here—what have you been cooking?"

I decided I wanted some vegetables and beef soup and—"

"Cornbread! Oh, how I have missed your cornbread!"

Later that evening, the two women sat out on the front porch in the old white rocking chairs, reminiscing of days of her youth. While Raylene is filling her mom in on everything she had learned about Kurt over these past months.

"You are a strong woman dear—I would be a basket case if all this was happening to me." Her mom reaches over and squeezes her hand. "What is your secret?"

Raylene blankly stares out in the distance for a while. What is her secret? What has given her strength? Then, finally, her eyes focus in on her dad's old truck, "God—and daddy. Watching him through the years—his strength—his endurance—he taught me to always trust in God to make things right—that has stuck with me all these years, and I have to believe that God is going to make this right."

"I have always wondered if the raising we gave you stuck." Her mom smiles lovingly, with a glow of pride on her face, "We tried hard to instill solid godly morals in you."

"It is those morals and values that has kept me sane all these years. In a strange way, I feel all this craziness is God's way of righting all these years of lies."

"What do you mean?"

"From day one of my relationship with Kurt—Trevor—it has all been a lie, mom." She turns sideways in her chair, pulling one leg up, and hugs it to her chest, "He lied about who he was—I was never told his real name. Our marriage was kept a secret to cover the lies he was keeping—Our daughter's birth was never filed with the courts. I find out he has a twin sister—who hates him for all he's done—it's like I don't even know the man I have been married to all these years—do you know how scary that is?"

"But then, I decide I don't want to live that life with him anymore—I told him I was leaving. He tried to kill me, and he has taken my daughter from me—but in the process all his secrets have come out into the open—in a way, I feel free—all I need is my daughter back, and my life would be complete." She hugs her knee tighter and smiles over at her mom, "I believe with everything in me, that my daughter will be home with me soon—God is going to bring her back to me."

Ruth wipes the tears that threaten her eyes, "I am so sorry that you have had to endure all these bad things. All this time, I thought you were happy. Why didn't you ever come to me—confide in me—that you were being treated this way by this awful man?"

"I didn't want to bother you, mom. We had just lost dad, and life just seemed to be moving in fast forward for me at the time." She sits up straight and moves to the edge of the chair, taking both of Ruth's hands in hers. "I'm sorry that I left you so soon after dad's passing. Looking back, I can see that was very selfish of me. I was excited about college and my future career—which I never got to finish—and Kurt—" she shakes her head, "He seemed so perfect in the beginning. I felt if I didn't hold onto him, that I would miss out on a great man—that's how convincing he was back then. I didn't see what he really was—and I will forever regret that. But I have become a stronger and wiser person for having endured that."

"You don't have to apologize to me for leaving so soon after your father's death. You did what you thought was right at that moment, and like I mentioned—you seemed so happy with Kurt—I thought you were happy— I'm sorry I didn't realize what was really going on in your life."

"When Liam told me all the things that they had uncovered about Kurt—I felt like such a fool. I knew something was off—but I never dreamed that the lies would be so—deleterious. He left me not knowing who I can trust. When I first met Liam and River—" she shakes her head in disbelief, "I was mean to them—and now—I can't imagine life without Liam, he is such a bounteous person. Why couldn't I have met him instead of Kurt?"

"Liam—huh?" her mom gives her a whimsical smile, "Sounds like you might be smitten by him."

"No! you have it all wrong—maybe I should reword that—why couldn't Kurt have been more like him?"

"Nothing ever happens by chance—there is a reason why God has sent Liam into your life—who knows what the future holds."

"Speaking of Liam—he's coming over early tomorrow morning—we're going to visit Brenda; she has agreed to meet with me. We're hoping she can help us get inside the mind of the real man I married—something that will help us figure out where Kurt can be hiding."

"I hope she is able to help—I know you want your daughter back with you—soon."

"That I do." She stands and gives her mom a hug, "I need to be getting to bed or I won't want to get up at such an ungodly hour—goodnight."

Ruth kisses her cheek, "Goodnight, dear."

****

Staring is rude—or at least that is what Raylene has always been taught. But she can't seem to take her eyes off Brenda. It is kind of eerie, actually—this woman is a female replica of her husband. Never in her life has she ever met fraternal twins that looked so much alike. It was almost whimsical. It was like looking at Kurt's face but with smoother skin, framed by long flowy hair.

Brenda's hate for her brother was evident in the venom that seemed to flow from her words as she spoke. Raylene couldn't help to wonder if it was true hate or disappointment in someone that looked so much like herself. She blinked her eyes and took a deep breath, trying to focus on what she is saying.

"Trevor wasn't always a troubled child. The problems didn't start until he was around fifteen or sixteen. Around that time, no matter what my parents did or gave—it never seemed to be enough for him. He started hanging around the wrong crowd—vandalizing—stealing—coming home drunk or stoned—you name it, he did it. They even tried sending him to a boarding school—it seemed to help for a while. But it was draining the family finances badly. They reached out to the state for help, but Trevor has always been good at putting up a good front. The state issued therapist didn't see any reason that he needed to be placed in a boarding school. So, help was denied."

Liam is the only one who seemed to be undeterred by this replica of her husband. Thank God, because he was the only one asking questions or commenting, "Did he ever get sent to juvenile detention?"

"Oh, yes. Several times actually."

"How old was he on the first trip?"

"He had just turned thirteen. He and a group of other boys robbed the gas station to buy drugs and beer."

"What kind of drugs were they doing?"

"Pot—of course, and meth. I don't know all the proper names, that's just what I recall hearing my dad tell my mom. He was in juvie twice for the same reasons. The last trip ended just before he turned eighteen. He seemed to do good for a short while. He stayed around home most of the time. Then he met this girl online and they started dating. We thought for sure he had decided to grow up and act better. But within six months of their courtship, he went into a jealous rage and put her in the hospital with broken ribs and a broken nose."

"Was he charged for that crime?" Liam darted his eyes to Raylene then back to Brenda.

"Yes, he got a five-year sentence. Of which he did one year in a state penitentiary down south. While out on parole, he met Beth Ann." She looks to Raylene as she says the woman's name. "Once again, he seemed to be on the right track—they got married—had a beautiful baby girl. Then when Ansley was—when we lost her—" she goes quiet for a moment. It is obvious that it is hard for her to speak of the death of her niece. "The drinking and drugging started back, and you know the rest—he almost killed Beth Ann—He did two years in prison for that and was out on parole when he killed my parents."

Liam looks over at Raylene, "Do you have any questions for Miss Sullivan?"

She clears her throat before trying to speak. "Do you have any idea how we can find where he is hiding my daughter? Anything thing at all that can help us find her?" she gives the woman a desperate stare.

"For almost nine years, I haven't as much as heard his name—much less have known that he was living in Chicago under my dad's identity. So, I assumed he had gone off somewhere and died. I know that seems cold, but that's that way it is—so, to answer your question—for your sake, I wish I could think of something—but, no, I don't have a clue where he could be hiding with your daughter—my niece." She adds the last part as she smiles sympathetically to Raylene.

They thanked her for agreeing to meet them and left their phone numbers just in case she should hear from him. As they drove away from the house, no one spoke for quite a while. Disappointment hangs in the air like an oppressive cloud. Threatening to suffocate any ray of hope they have on finding Nylah.

"We know no more than we did before we came," Raylene is the first to speak, "What do we do now?"

"We keep searching," Liam reaches over and squeezes her hand, "We keep searching until we find them—giving up is not a choice. He's out there somewhere—and even if it's the last thing I do—I am going to search until I have your daughter back with you."

Chapter 9
Trevor (Kurt)

The acorn sounded like a gunshot blast as it hit the hollow tin roof of the barn, Trevor bolted up right, the hay he was sleeping on clinging to his hair. It took him a minute to get his bearings and realize where he was. What was he thinking when he decided to come here? The last time he had spoken to his sister, she was beyond livid with him. But she is his last hope for getting help with Nylah. He doesn't know the first thing about taking care of a child. Bringing her with him was a mistake, but when he came to and Raylene was nowhere to be found, only a trail of blood leading out the front door—he couldn't leave her alone. It could have been days before anyone found her there.

Feeling like he didn't have a choice, he had quickly run up the stairs and retrieved her from her bed—grabbing the bag that her mom had already packed to take her away. What was she thinking when she decided to leave? Did she really think he would just let her walk out of his life? And after everything he has done to protect her. He never told her about his past, because somethings are better left unsaid—she should have just trusted him. All the times they had fought and all the times he had hit her—all she had to do was stop questioning him, stop nagging him about things she didn't understand.

He was always telling her that he was only protecting her. 'Protecting me from what or who?' she would always ask. Things didn't have to end like this. *Do you see it now Raylene? Do you understand now what I was trying to protect you from? Now the truth is out. Now they know who I really am, and they won't stop until they find me. And when they do, they will lock me away, for very a long time.*

He looks at the sleeping child lying just feet from him. She'll be waking up soon, and Brenda will be coming out at any time to tend to the cows and get the farm started up for the day. He doesn't want her to find them this way.

So, he quietly stands and peers down at his daughter—the daughter who has lived in his house all her life—the daughter whom he knows nothing about—the daughter who only knows him as the mean man that yells at mommy. Over these past two months, he regrets how he has refused to be part of her life; but what was he to do? Deep inside, he always feared this day would come. From the beginning, he knew he couldn't live this lie forever. Yet, he knew that someday, somehow, the truth would come out.

Now here it is, and he has no choice but to try to right his wrongs. Raylene must be out of her mind with worry right now. But this is all her fault. *Now we can't be together—but hey, that's what she wanted anyway—making up some lie about going to stay with her mother! I thought her parents were dead—at least I assumed. I had told her that family was dead to us; all we needed was each other—just me and her. First, she goes and has a kid—I told her I didn't want kids. Then she wouldn't shut up about my family—why is she so persistent in finding out about my family? Some things are just better left in the past—and my family is one of them. Now here I am having to reach out to my sister for help, all because Raylene couldn't leave well enough alone.*

A ray of sun broke through a crack just over his head, casting a dusty bean across Nylah's face. Brenda will be out soon. If he wants to talk with her at the house, he'd better head there now. He doesn't want to be discovered like this. Pushing the door open slowly, he makes his way out of the barn and across the yard. It had been dark when they arrived last night. He had taken the trail road down by the creek so he could hide his car. Although it had been years since he set foot on the property, everything seemed to be the same.

At least his sister had worked hard to keep the place going. It still looks good to be so old. Everything was still in place, as if the family was all still together. Even his mom's flower beds, which she loved so much, were just as she had left them. He never took his sister for the flowering kind. But she has done a great job. He skips up the steps and knocks on the front door; Brenda appears almost immediately.

"Oh, no—no, no, no—Trevor what are you doing here?" she reaches beside the door, and in a swift moment, Trevor is looking down the barrel of a shotgun, "Get off my property—now!"

"Brenda, please! I have my daughter with me, I need your help. Her mother—"

"Her mother what? Kicked y'all out?" she raises the gun to point right between his eyes, "I don't want to hear all your lies, Trevor! I know the truth; the cops have already been here looking for you. I know what you have done. For goodness' sake, what is wrong with you?"

"Brend—"

"Don't say my name—you're dead to me already." She nudges the gun close to his face.

Taking a step back, he makes one last attempt to plead with his sister, "Please, I know I have messed up. Just help me make this right. I shouldn't have brought her with me, I just didn't know what to do. Her mama just ran out the door and I didn't know if she was coming back for her. I couldn't just leave her there."

"Her *mama* didn't just run out Trevor—you tried to kill her! She left the house to get help! And how dare you to steal my daddy's name—and job!"

He glared at his sister in shock—they know—they know everything. Which means Raylene knows. All his secrets of the past nine years have all been revealed. "They know?"

"Yes, Trevor—we all know what you have done. I always wondered how you managed to stay hid all this time. Now I know—and I desperately despise you for being so low—now please leave."

"I'm planning on taking her back to her mom—my daughter. She needs a good bath and a change of clothes—and a decent meal." He shoves his hands in pockets, stares at a small pebble stuck in the boards of the porch; "Don't do it for me—do it for her—please." He hated to use the kid, but that's the only thing he has at the time. The truth was—he needed those things just as badly. And if the cops have been here recently, they won't come back anytime soon—unless his sister calls them. He'd just have to keep a close eye on her for a few days—just to get his thoughts together on what to do next.

Brenda glances towards the barn just in time to see the little girl coming out the door, rubbing her eyes. She lowers the gun and sits it just inside the door. Trevor follows her eyes to find his daughter has awaken and is heading towards them.

"Please" he pleads one last time to his sister.

She lets out a loud sigh, "Go get her and bring her inside. I will run her a bath, get her cleaned up and fed—then I want you out of here—and take her straight back to her mama."

She turns and walks inside the house not giving him a chance to answer. He waits on Nylah to approach and leads her inside the house. Trevor was surprised at what his sister had done to the place. It was the same—but different. She had updated the walls, furniture, flooring and curtains. But it still has a homey feel about it.

"It looks great around here sis—you've done great at keeping it up."

"Don't call me sis—I am no longer *sis* to you." She whispers aggressively so that the girl doesn't hear. "I'll need your help around here today. I have called the farm hands and gave them the day off. Most of them know you—so plan on staying long enough to help get all this work done today."

He nodded in response. Suddenly he couldn't seem to find his words. It cut deep to have his sister so bitter towards him. They were once so close. Why couldn't she be more understanding about his circumstances? Just like Raylene, she couldn't see it either. All people seemed to see is all the bad he had done—what about all the bad that has happened to him? Why can't they understand that the decisions he had made was due to all those terrible things? People knew he had a bad temper—so, why did they do things to set it off. Beth Ann let his daughter get killed—of course he wasn't thinking straight when he did those things to her. The drinking problem—that was because of losing his child because he left her alone with a careless mother—sleeping instead of keeping an eye on her—she let her die! He met Raylene—he finally had a second chance to get it right. So that is why he had to lie about who he was. His dad passing away opened a new life for him and he took it—was that so bad? It's only bad because that woman—he loves her so much that he would take on someone else's identity to be with her—but she had to go and ruin it all. She ran out on them—leaving him with the daughter he never wanted. But everyone looks at him as if he is the bad guy—*What about me?*

He could hear the water running in the tub in the bathroom; walking to the door, he could hear Brenda talking sweet and loving to the kid. *Is that the way you are supposed to talk to them? No wonder she wouldn't speak to me. I suppose I was a little bit too gruff for her.* He taps on the door as he pops his head in, "I'm going to get started on this work around here—will you be alright with her?" he nods toward Nylah.

"Do you remember what to do on a farm?"

"Of course, si—um—yes I remember well. I did it more than you for the first half of my life."

"Well then, go get started—me and little missy will be just fine—going to get her cleaned up and fed, and then I'll bring her out to see the cow and horses." She fakes a smile to her brother.

Trevor knew it was fake too; but it felt good to have her smile at him again. It seems like forever since his sister had done anything but snarl at him. How could they have once been so close and so inseparable—and now seem so far apart? He shook his head to clear his thoughts as he headed out into the barn. This is going to be a rough day—it has been a lifetime since he had to do farm work.

****

"I can't believe you got all that work done so fast—and all by yourself." Brenda mused as she set a plate in front of her brother. "I know it's been a good twenty years since you've helped out around here."

"Some things you just never forget." He thanked her for the food as she places it in front of him, "Hey, thanks for helping me with the ki—my daughter. I really appreciate what you are doing." He looks around into the living room, "Where is she anyway?"

"I've tucked her in for the night. Me and her had a busy day." She gave a soft laugh, "It's been fun having a little one around."

"So—I-I thought we were leaving as soon as I was done?"

"That little girl needs a good night's sleep. I figured—"

"Figured?"

"Y'all can stay here for tonight—I put her in my old room, I made yours for you—I have taken mom and dad's old room." She pours him some more black coffee, "But—one night is all I can give you."

For a moment the room was silent.

"What happened to us Trevor?" Brenda was the one to break the silence, "What happened to you? We used to be so happy together—you were happy. Where did it all go wrong?"

He took time to choose his words wisely. Now wasn't the time to say the wrong thing—he'd just tell her what she wants to hear. At least that would buy them a good night's rest in a warm bed—he knows his sister well—she'd have no problem kicking them out if he should say the wrong thing."

"I really don't know—grew tired of small-town living—got bored." He shoves another bite of buttery homemade buttermilk biscuit in his mouth. "Biscuits are delicious—they taste just like mamas." He threw in before continuing. "If I had to guess—I'd say that high school was when it started—I got into the wrong crowd. I just wanted to—run—I often wonder how things would have been different if I'd made better choices."

"Take that baby to her mama, Trevie."

Trevor stops chewing and swallows the bite of biscuit before it's fully chewed. It has been years since he'd heard her call him by that name. It had been years since his sister had even remotely said something so enduring to him.

"Promise me—right now—that when you leave here, you will take her straight to her mama. That's all she talked about today—she wants her mom."

"I have people watching the house—she not there, and they have no idea where she went. So—I'll have to find her before I can do that, but that is my intentions."

Brenda sits back in her chair, stares blankly at her feet under the table. A lot of years have passed, but he knows his sister well enough to know there's something she's not telling him. "What?" He pushes the plate to the side and props his elbow on the table, "Tell me what you are thinking—right now."

His sister lets out a breath before beginning, "Raylene and some detective came by here a few days ago."

"And?"

"I don't' know if I should tell you anymore that— how do I know what your intentions are? I don't mean to sound so distrusting—but how do I know that you aren't looking to harm this lady?"

"I swear to you, Brenda—I only want to right these wrongs."

She closes her eyes as if pondering on the decision, "Okay, I'll tell you." She began as she leans in on the table, "She's at her mama's house in Blue Ridge—I don't know the address, but it shouldn't be hard to find her in a small town like that."

"Blue Ridge huh? I'll look into that and see what I can find out."

She looks at her brother suspiciously, "You don't want to know why she was here? Or what was said?"

"No—she's looking for her daughter. And if I know Raylene—she will stop at nothing to find us. I'll just have to find her first and give her back what she wants."

They sat and talked for an hour more before he rose to head to bed. As he stands in front of the bathroom mirror, staring at his reflection. Thoughts of his childhood, filled with mixed emotions flood over him. Oh, how he wishes he could go back in time and change things—this time, he meant it, and the thought scares him. His worst mistake was holding on to the anger caused by his teenage disobedience. That was where he made his first mistake—he purposefully chose to hang out with kids he knew his daddy would hate—all because he didn't want to be told what to do. Those kids had introduced him to a life that would change everything forever.

Brenda had asked about his anger—his true anger was at himself. How could he tell her that? Once the drugs and alcohol took control of his life, it was too late to go back. He couldn't stop—he hated himself for that. It was then that he became a very discontented person. No matter how hard he tries, he has never been able to get away from it—even now—but no one knows. The sound of his sister's voice seeping through the walls brings him out of his thoughts.

"I told them they could stay for tonight—I don't know—no, wait until tomorrow morning—but come early, I don't know what time he'll be leaving."

She's setting me up! My own sister is trying to trap me and send me away to prison—why? I only asked for her help, and this is what she is doing to me? He slowly opens the bathroom door and quietly walks down the hallway to his room. He waits until he hears her go into the bedroom on the other side of the house. He gathers his things and tiptoes in to awake Nylah, "We need to go sweetie. We've got to go to mommy—she's waiting for us. But you must be very quiet because Aunt Brenda is sleeping, and we don't want to wake her."

He quickly gathers her things and carries her out the backdoor. They make their way around the barn and out across the field to the trail road on the back of the property. As he places her inside the car—making sure she is secure in the back seat—he closes the door and takes one last look back across the field; all that is visible is a tiny dim porch light—home—but he knows this will be the last time he will ever be on these grounds. He now knows that there is nothing left here for him. *She tried to betray me—but by the time they arrive—I'll be long gone!*

Goodbye, sis—forever.

Chapter 10
River

Standing on the porch waiting for someone to come to the door, River wondered if she should have asked what was considered early. 6 am seemed like the appropriate decision—early—but not too early, at least to her. She supposed everybody had a difference in opinion on what that time could be. Through the sheer curtain, she could see the shadow of Brenda Sullivan heading towards the door. She tugs at her shirttail and dusts off nonexistent debris from its front, straightens her five-foot-two frame to appear taller for when the door opens.

"Hi, Miss Sullivan—I hope I'm not too early." She whispers as the door opens.

"Please—just Brenda, and—" Brenda begins as she pushes past her instead of inviting her inside. "Obviously not early enough," she states frantically, "They're not here!"

She heads off the porch and nearly runs towards the barn. River stands perplexed for a moment. Then, not knowing what to do, she follows the woman across the yard.

"What do you mean they are not here?" she calls out as she races to catch up with her, "When did they leave? I have—Brenda—can we stop for a minute?" She reaches out and lightly tugs her arm as Brenda starts back towards the house. "Take a deep breath and tell me what happened."

"I don't know—I suppose he decided to leave with that child in the middle of the night—Why I don't know. He didn't even leave a note." Brenda scans the property, umbrellaing her eyes to look out across the field.

"What are the chances that they just went out for something?"

"At 6 am? What is open at this hour? Trevor loves my cooking—so he wouldn't be going out to buy food, that's how I discovered they were gone—I went to let him know breakfast was ready." She shrugs her shoulders, "This is just like him—I wonder if he heard me on the phone last night?

River took out her cell phone and hit the call button, "Call them off—he's not here, during the night she thinks—just discovered herself—okay." She ends the call and turns back to Brenda.

"Did he happen to say anything about what his plans might be?"

"Only that he should have never brought the little girl with him—and he wants to get her back to her mama." Pointing at the phone she adds, "What was that about?"

"A few officers were waiting up on the road for my cue to apprehend him—I just had them sent away. My partner is on his way here, do you think we can sit down together and see if maybe he said something that might give us an idea on where he may be headed?"

Brenda answers with a nod and turns to lead her to the house. Just as they reach the door, an unmarked car comes up the driveway to drop off Liam. River waits until her partner joins her before she enters the house.

She leans in close to him to whisper, "Looks like he has out-smarted us again."

"I'm going to find him—he best have his fun while he can."

She knows her partner well enough to know that Liam Geoffrey has a personal vendetta to find Trevor and get that little girl back to her mom. She couldn't help but wonder how personal this is for him; the two of them have worked together for over ten years now. River can't remember a time that her partner has ever gotten this close to a client before. He knows it's not an intelligent thing to do. A lot of trouble could come from this. Getting personally involved always brought problems—Liam knows this. He's the one who warned her of such things when she took the job with him.

She turns her attention back to Brenda, as she takes a seat at the kitchen table, "Brenda, if you could just go over the last conversation you and Trevor had last night—

maybe there is something there that might tell us where he may be headed."

"The last thing we spoke about was him taking that baby to her mama."

"Did he say when he was planning to do this?"

Brenda shook her head, "No time soon I'd guess— he had asked to stay here a few days—I only allowed him the one night." She looks from one to the other before continuing, "I wanted to turn him in—I was only trying to help. I don't know what happened, I really don't."

Liam was the next to respond, but more to River than Brenda, "You mentioned that he said he plans to take Nylah back to Raylene—I need to get someone at that house. If he arrives and no one is there—we may lose track of him again."

"Wait—that reminds me," Brenda leans in on the table, "that's what we last talked about—I told him—" her words trail off, and she stares at the floor beside the table.

"You told him what?" River shoots a wary look at Liam.

"I told him—Raylene is in Blue Ridge Georgia with her mama." She shrugs and gives them an apologetic smile.

Liam left the chair so fast that it almost toppled over. He takes out his phone as he heads for the front door, "I'm sorry, but we've got to get to her—now! We don't know what this man's intentions are. I don't want Raylene to be caught unaware if he should show up there."

River apologizes to her as they head for the car. Then, after thanking her for her help and time—they were on the road.

****

They drove the better part of an hour in silence. River had contemplated turning the radio on, but she knew they would only end up turning it right back off. They always did their best brainstorming in silence. If only she knew what he was thinking about at the moment. She wanted so desperately to warn him about how close he was getting to this woman.

Out the corner of her eye, she could see him flexing the muscles in his jaw—something he did when determination was driving him. The two of them go way back to elementary school. Liam had married her best friend—and she had married his. The four of them were inseparable. But, after high school and college, life had taken them in different directions.

Mark had taken a job in Texas soon after they married. Leaving Lisa and Liam behind was the hardest thing for them to do—but all that was on their young minds was the money that was to be made and the freedom to get out of Georgia. So, with stars in their eyes, they had set out on their new life—Mark, a big shot attorney, and she a beat-cop.

After Mark's death, she had been devastated. Often hiding away in a lonely, dark house in her pajamas and not bathing for days, eating next to nothing. Needless to say—

111

her five-year career ended. Who wants to keep a cop on that is never on the beat? She found herself being evicted from her home, with no job—her physical appearance had gone from lean and healthy—to a skeleton covered in skin, with sunken eyes—and then she had gotten the call that her best friend since kindergarten was lost to her in death.

It was that phone call that saved her life. Making her way back to Georgia, she found Liam sinking in the same darkness. Only he handled it differently—instead of hiding away in doom and gloom—he engrossed himself with work. Taking on more cases than he could handle turned out to be an open door for River. He needed a partner, and she needed a job.

The ringing of the phone lying beside her on the seat quickly brought her out of her thoughts. Hitting the call button, she raises it to her ear, "Detective River—" she lets out a gasp, "That completely slipped my mind— no, just have her wait, I'll can be there in twenty minutes."

She glances over at Liam, who is now staring at her with a confused look on his face as she throws the phone down between them, "I'm sorry," she says to him, "We're going to have to make a detour and a plan change."

"What's going on?" she can see the agitation on Liam's face and knows he is unhappy with the delay getting to Raylene.

"Remember the Soranto account?"

Liam answers with a nod and motions for her to continue.

"Mrs. Soranto is coming in today for us to go over the findings—I'm sorry, but I forgot they have court tomorrow morning—this has to be done today." She rushes ahead, not giving him time to object, "I have to be in court with them. So, you are going to have to make this trip by yourself—did I say I'm sorry?" She shoots a smile in his direction.

They pull into the parking lot; Liam exits before the car has been placed in park. "Just leave it running—I need to get on the road—time is running out."

She steps out of the car and watches as he hurries into the driver's seat, and speeds out into traffic, then turning, she walks towards the redbrick building that is their office in Georgia. She shakes her head at his desperate actions—*yeah, he is definitely in way over his head.* If only she could be there with him now. Watching the two of them together was amusing, with the way they both are in denial of their feelings for each other.

As she walks towards the office, she tries to clear her mind and focus on the case at hand. The Soranto's had hired her last year to investigate an employee they suspected was embezzling money from their company. Those suspicions had proven to be right. So, she must clear her mind of Liam and Raylene, for now at least.

A movement by the office entry causes her to stop in her tracks. Why is someone standing at the office door? She reaches inside her blazer and unsnaps the gun from the holster—best to have it ready in case these people are up to no good.

"Can I help you?" she yells once they are in view.

As they turn and walk towards her, she can see a man and a woman. Apparently, a couple—the way the woman is holding onto the man's arm.

"We're sorry to bother you miss," the man begins, "We're looking for Detective Geoffrey."

"I'm sorry but you just missed him." She points out into the traffic on the street, "I'm Detective Donaldson—his partner. Is there something I can assist you with?"

"My name is Wyatt—Wyatt Kapers, and this here is my wife, Sarah."

River cautiously walks closer. Hearing the names put her on edge. What do they want with Liam? Hopefully, they have come to tell them where Kurt is hiding.

"We just want to tell Ms. Sullivan that we meant her no harm—figured the detective to get that message to her."

"Okay—I can tell her for you." River knew this might be her only chance to get information out of them—too bad she had a court date awaiting her. "Are you sure you don't know where Mr. Sullivan is hiding?" she chose to be direct.

"N-no ma'am. I really wish we could help find that little girl. He seems to have just vanished. Th-The last time he called, he only said he was going away for a while, and he wanted us to keep track of Raylene."

For the first time, his wife speaks, "But of course—we haven't been doing that. We really didn't know the truth behind Mr. Sullivan. He made us believe that he was afraid that she would leave him and take his daughter away—said that she was crazy and needed to be watched with the child."

"But after meeting Mrs. Sullivan, we now know that ain't true." Wyatt finished for his wife.

River can feel the sincerity behind the couple's words. "Thank you for wanting to apologize for you actions. I will pass this on to Mrs. Sullivan."

As she walks into the office, she dials Liam and tells him what just happened. "Looks like Mr. Sullivan just keeps losing all his friends." She says to him.

She rushes off the phone to gather her paperwork for court. But unfortunately, she is going to have to hurry if she plans to make it on time.

Chapter 11

Raylene

Before the phone finishes the first ring, Raylene is out of the chair and dashing for the kitchen. *It's about time Liam calls,* she thinks to herself. She reaches it just as the second ring ends, "Hello," she answers enthusiastically.

"Hello—w-who—Kurt!" Her body begins to tremble at the sound of his voice, "How did you—" He hung up before she had time to finish her sentence.

Just as she places the phone back on the wall, she hears a car pull up to the house. Peering out the window, she sees Liam exit and starts towards the porch. Frantically, she races out to him.

"Kurt—he called—just now—he called!"

Liam rushes to her, holding her tight against him; he can feel her body tremble, "Calm down—Raylene— tell me calmly what happened." He tries to console her.

Feeling embarrassed by her actions, she pushes away from him as she leads him into the house before she tries to speak again, allowing herself to calm down a little.

"The phone rang," she begins as she tries to hide the tremble in her voice, "I thought it was you calling with an update on Kurt. But it was him—how did he get this number? How does he know I'm here?" she questioned more to herself than to Liam.

"What did he say?" Liam leans in closer, hating to tell her just yet that Brenda told him where she was. "Did you ask where he was? Did he say or give a hint of his whereabouts?" he knew it was unprofessional to ramble questions so fast, but this had become personal to him. He wants to find this man more than he would like to admit.

"No. He didn't give me time to speak or ask questions. He only said—" she paused as the tremors of fear rose once more inside her body, "He said—*Do you see what you've done now—you will pay dearly for this—* then he hung up."

"Narcissistic people make me sick." Liam stands and starts to pace the small kitchen. "He brought all this on—yet he wants to put the blame on you."

"It's okay, I'm use to him doing this—he always has—with everything."

"Look, I've got bad news and I don't know if you and your mom need to stay here." He couldn't look at her as he spoke these words. The feeling that he has somehow failed to keep her safe keeps gnawing at him.

"I don't see how him calling here could be a problem—he has the phone number, not the address." The realization of him being a cop suddenly shows in her eyes. "If he has the number—he could have somehow gotten the address too though—right?" she looks to Liam searchingly.

"If he somehow found out you were here—yes, he could look up the name and number and find the address. But—" He pauses before continuing. "—that is why I rushed here."

"I was wondering about that—you said you would call, but I knew something was wrong when I saw you outside. What happened? And be honest with me."

"I should have called, but I—"

"Tell me Liam!"

"We—me and River—got a call that he was at Brenda's."

"And?" she urged him on.

"He had asked to stay there for a few days. But our guess is that when Brenda called to tell River about him being there—he heard." He sits back down at the table, places his elbows on his knees, and buries his face in his hands.

"What does that mean exactly—that doesn't explain how he got my number and address—" Raylene joined him at the table as realization hit. "I gave Brenda my number—did she give my number to Kur—Trevor?"

"Not exactly what happened." Liam sits up straight and turns to face her, "she told him you were here—at your mom's house. My guess is that he got your number from her refrigerator door. However, he can look up the number online and get the address."

"Why would she tell him I am here?" Raylene leans back in the chair as she shakes her head, "I don't understand why she would do that. Brenda—of all people—knows how he is."

"You know how convincing he can be—look at how he did you over these nine years. Trevor probably gave her some sad story about wanting to bring Nylah back to you—you know—do the right thing kind of story."

Nodding in agreement, Raylene inhales and exhales loudly. "So—what do we do now?" she was beginning to feel defeated with this entire situation. Wanting her daughter to be returned—but at the same time trying to stay under Trevor's radar. What is she supposed to do? Have a standoff with him, or keep running from him?

His words on the phone kept echoing through her mind—*Do you see what you've done now—you will pay dearly for this.* It's clear that he isn't ready to make amends. He is doing what he always does, trying to intimidate her to get his way.

Liam walks over to the coffee pot, "Do you mind?" he asks as he takes a cup from the cabinet.

"Yes, of course. I'm so sorry I haven't offered it to you before now."

He fills the cup and returns to the table, "I suggest you let me find somewhere for you and your mom to stay." He finally answers after taking a sip of hot coffee.

"No." Raylene answers quickly, "I'm not running from him anymore—and mom would never agree to leaving her home."

"Okay then—I'll stay here with the two of you." He stated sternly.

"You would have to sleep on the sofa."

"Looks like I'm sleep on the sofa then, doesn't it?"

****

Waking to the smell of bacon frying downstairs, Raylene rolls over to glance at the clock on the bedside table. *Mom has always been an early riser—but since when does she cook breakfast at 4:30 am?* She throws back the covers and stretches as she sits on the bed; sliding her feet into her house shoes, she heads for the bathroom to get dressed.

Usually, she would go down in her nightclothes but seeing that they have a houseguest. Getting a shower and getting dressed seems the best choice. She examines the face smiling back at her from the mirror. Those dark circles are going to be hard to cover. It seems to take her forever to fall asleep, then once she does, Nylah's cries in her dreams prevent her from resting. *God, I am trying to stay strong and trust that you are keeping her safe; but I need her back with me—this is killing me, and I don't know how much longer I can remain strong without her.*

Raylene's smile has faded; she stares at the sad eyes in the mirror for just a second, then she starts to attempt to cover the evidence of the recent events from her face. *Makeup can only cover up so much,* she whispers to her reflection. Then running a brush through her hair, she dresses and turns to go downstairs. *I can't wait to find out what mom is cooking.*

Tiptoeing down the stairs, she enters the living room and looks towards the sofa—Where has Liam gone so early? "Mom did Liam—" she freezes in mid-sentence as she enters the kitchen. Liam, and not her mom, is adding the last pancake to the top of a stack, "Liam—Hi," she looks around confused as she ponders on what he is doing up so early—cooking pancakes and bacon.

"Where's mom?" she finally asks, "And why are you cooking breakfast at this hour?"

"I couldn't sleep—so I thought I'd get breakfast started," he waves the spatula over the feast set out on the table. He has not only cooked pancakes and bacon; there are eggs, grits, and coffee as well. "My guess your mom is still sleeping," He adds as she walks around the table, admiring the spread laid out before her.

"You know you didn't have to do this—right?"

"I know—I wanted to—after all, I sort of invited myself to stay here—it's the least I can do to pay for my keep while I'm here." He turns and looks at her, "Do you realize that in all the confusion yesterday—you never told me your mom's name—I've just been calling her ma'am."

"I would never even think about making you earn your keep." Startled, Liam and Raylene turn, just as her mom enters the kitchen, "and my name is Irene Florence." She smiles across the table at him as she takes a seat, "The food smells and looks delicious."

Liam and Raylene stare at the woman for a few seconds before taking a seat at the table themselves.

"Thanks Mrs. Florence—"

"Irene—call me Irene. Could you pass the syrup please?" she sneaks a smile to her daughter as Liam passes the syrup across the table.

Raylene feels her cheeks burn. She knows her face has turned a bright red. Why would her mom smile at her like that? Does she think the two of them prepared this meal together?

"Wasn't it nice for Liam to get up so early and fix breakfast for us mom?" she begins in her defense, "I came downstairs expecting to find you—only to find Liam instead." She returns the sly smile to her mom. This is not the Irene she is used to. Raylene can't remember when her mom has ever approved of any boy who had tried to date her.

From the moment she met Kurt, she did not like him. Always telling Raylene that *the boy is too secretive, I don't trust him.* Raylene thought it was just her mom being mom, always making it seem like no one was worthy of her daughter. But looking back now, she wishes she had listened. Irene had been right about *the boy.* But look what a mess she had gotten herself into by not listening.

She steals a glance at Liam; what is it about this one that mom seems to have forgotten that he is here helping her find her daughter—that has been taken by her *husband.* Irene, of all people, should understand that a married woman couldn't go chasing after another man. Even if that woman is married to a lying lunatic.

Liam is everything her mom used to loathe in the boys of her past. His hair is always a mess, his slacks are not press, his shirt is wrinkled—then there's the haphazard way he tucks it into slacks. Kurt was everything her mom should have adored—but no—she seems to now approve of imperfection in a man. Raylene glances once more to Liam, *this perfectly imperfect man,* she thinks to herself.

She looks up to find her mom staring at, "Mom, your food is getting cold." She didn't know exactly what that look means; knowing her mother, it could be anything.

"I seem to have lost my appetite since you arrived." Irene smiles over to her daughter.

"I'm sorry. I didn't know my presence did that to you." Raylene jokingly responded.

"Lord, no. I just can't believe you are here—sitting at my table enjoying this delicious meal."

Raylene admires this woman more than anything. She took in the way the sunlight, coming through the window behind her, makes her silver hair sparkle like diamonds. Still beautiful after all these years. However, she can't help but wonder if the wrinkles on her face were put there by her. Being away from Nylah has opened her eyes to how deep a mother's love really is. Every day that her daughter is away makes her heartbreak even more.

Is that what Irene has been feeling? Has every day away from her daughter over these past nine years aged her that much more? Phone calls and facetime are good ways to keep in touch, but has her mom needed more than that? Nothing can replace physical contact.

As she glances once more at her mom, a movement outside the window catches her attention. "Someone's out there," she says as she pushes back her chair and stands to get a better view. "Kurt!" she shouts as she reaches across the table to her mom.

"Raylene, he's not here." Liam rushes to pull her off the table. "Remember the park?"

She tries to wiggle free of Liam's grasp, "He has a gun! Get down mom!"

"Oh, good grief Raylene," her mom says as she stands to walk toward the window, "It's probably the neighbor's dog."

Raylene lets out an ear-piercing scream as the window shatters seconds after the gun fires. Irene freezes, then falls backward, hitting her head on the table as she goes down.

"Call 911!" Liam yells as he reaches for the gun he has tucked in the waistband of his slacks, "and check on your mom," he adds as he dashes out the door.

Raylene grabs the phone off the wall and dials for emergency as she rushes to her mom. Blood is already pooling on the floor. As the dispatcher answers, Raylene states her name and address as she runs to get towels from the hall closet. Then she does as the dispatcher tells her, she folds the towels and locates the gushing blood wound, placing the towel on top, and applies as much pressure as she can.

"Mom, stay awake," she looks down at her pale face, the face that was just rosy and glowing. How can Kurt be so heartless?

The voice on the phone is asking her questions. "Yes, I know who did this—no he's not, he ran—Liam— Detective Liam Geoffrey is here—he ran after him— where is the ambulance—no, I don't hear them yet." Finally, after a few minutes and many questions, "I hear them—thank you." She ends the call and yells for the EMT to hurry.

She watches helplessly as they work with her mom, and place her on the gurney, and slide her into the back of the ambulance.

"Are you riding with us?" one of the EMTs asks her.

"I-I guess," she answers as she looks around the property, "Has anyone locate Detective Geoffrey yet?"

"No, we are still searching the area for him and Mr. Sullivan." A police officer standing nearby answers her. "If you don't mind, we will meet you at the hospital to ask some questions."

"Okay," Raylene answers weakly as she slowly climbs up into the back with her mom. She hates the thought of leaving Liam behind, but her mom needs her more.

****

The next few hours seem to go by so slowly; it doesn't help that Raylene keeps looking at the clock every few seconds. Shouldn't her mom be out of surgery by now? The doctor had told her it would be two to three hours. Instead, it's going on four. Still, she can't help but think that this is all her fault. What was she thinking when she decided to visit her mom? Kurt had never asked about her hometown, never even asked about her parents. Now, her mom is in surgery, having a bullet removed, and getting repairs on her abdomen. It's all because Raylene put her in this situation.

She closes her eyes and starts to pray, *God, I don't know if you can hear me right now—I feel so far from you. But please help my mom—I don't understand why all these things are happening to me. I don't know where my daughter is. That monster has her. And now he has hurt my mom. I finally get a chance to visit with her—and this happens.* Raylene opens her eyes and looks around the empty waiting room. It seems like no one else in this small-town, needs emergency surgery today. Usually, this place is buzzing this time of day. *Why do I have to be going through this right now? Why can't it be someone else?*

Raylene looks towards the brightly lit ceiling. *I'm sorry, I know that is selfish of me—I don't wish this on anyone. Please keep everyone safe—my mom, Nylah, and Liam—wherever he is.* And where is Liam? She has tried calling his phone several times, and no answer. Even had called River too and left a message. So far, she has heard from no one. All the police station is telling her is they are still looking for him. "Where are you?" she says out loud to the empty room.

"I'm right here?"

The voice startles her, and she rises as the doctor walks over to greet her.

"I'm sure I'm not the one you were looking for—but I'm here with news on your mother—I'm certain that is something you are also wanting to hear." He smiles at her.

He's smiling, so he must have good news, Raylene thinks to herself as she nods for the doctor to continue.

"The surgery went a little longer than we anticipated; the bullet has been extracted. However, there is extensive damage to a few of her internal organs, mainly her large intestine, we had to remove a portion of it. She is in recovery right now; her vitals are awesome, and she should be awake soon—do you have any questions so far?"

"A lot—actually. But first—is she going to have any long-term issues from this?

"We won't know the answer to that for a few days now. However, most people don't have any issues with this type of surgery." He pauses to wait for her next question.

"When can I see her?"

"A nurse will be coming shortly to take you to a room upstairs—we are going to keep her for a few days to make sure there are no other internal issues that we may have missed."

"What do you mean you may have missed?"

"This kind of injuries can be a little tricky. Sometimes we may miss a spot since it's not bleeding at the time of surgery. Then later it can start back up and cause problems that we will have to go back in and fix. We always hope for the best in these situations and try to do everything we can to avoid this happening."

Raylene remained silent, trying to take in all the doctor had just told her.

"Do you have any more questions for me?"

"No—not right now." She smiles as she takes the doctor's outreached hand. "Thank you for all you have done."

"No thanks required—and I hope you find whoever it is you looking for." He returns her smile as he turns to leave.

A few minutes later, a nurse comes and escorts her upstairs to wait for her mom. While she sits there, alone once again, her mind wanders back to her life before Kurt. She and her parents once had a close relationship. Raylene was a hard-core daddy's girl for day one. But she and her mom had always been close too. When her dad passed away, trying to get her mom to move to Chicago had been a failure. She had only laughed at Raylene. Georgia Blue Ridge Mountains were her home and would always be.

Raylene shakes off the thoughts as she reaches for her cell phone; finding Liam's number, she tries it once more. Still no answer. She didn't leave a message this time. After all, she had already left a dozen or more throughout the day. Too many messages may make her seem desperate. She smiles at the thought of being desperate—caring for people seems to make you that way—and she does care desperately about Liam's wellbeing. *I hate not knowing if you are safe. Did you catch Kurt? Did he have Nylah? Or*—the thought she hated thinking the most—*has he hurt both of you instead?*

With everything she has come to find out about her husband, Raylene doesn't know what to think. From what she has learned, he has hurt a lot of people from a very young age. His rage has always been something to be feared—never knowing what might set him off, she always tried to stay silent, trying to read his mood. Sometimes it didn't matter what she did, he always seemed to be angry—but at what she never knew. That's a mystery that will probably never be solved.

Her only hope is that they will get him before he hurts someone else. He has taken so much of her life from her—she prays he doesn't take Nylah and Liam too.

■■■

Chapter 12
Liam

The gnarled roots dipping in and out of the ground made the journey through the forest a challenge as Liam ran back towards the house. The twisted branches of the trees reached down, like fingers grasping thin air, slapping him in the face and tearing at his clothes. The melting snow didn't help much either. Although its raw, earthy scent filled the air, knowing exactly where the muddy spots would appear made his trek difficult. But he had to get back to the house—to his car.

He hates that he had to leave Raylene like that. He has no way of knowing how badly her mom was hurt—or even if she is still alive. *Raylene is probably upset that I abandoned her. But I had him in my sight for a good way through the forest.* As he pushes through the last of the branches, he picks up his speed as he runs across the yard and into the house to retrieve his keys and cellphone. Raylene is no doubt going out of her mind wondering where he is. But he must first try and catch up to Trevor.

Once in his car, he dials Ronny's number. He filled him in on what had happened with Raylene's mom and about the chase through the woods. "He won't get far. I got a good shot at him—no in the leg, I wasn't trying to kill him—No—he still managed to get away. However, I did get the tag and make of the car he's driving—Midnight blue Honda Pilot—Georgia plates."

After filling him in on all the details, Liam calls the hospital when he doesn't get an answer on Raylene's phone. Jotting down the room number, he throws the phone in the seat beside him and speeds out onto the main road. He must get to her. Trevor no doubt knows where she is and may try to go there. It wouldn't be a smart thing for him to do—but none of Trevor's actions lately have been smart ones. *Even though he seems to always outsmart us,* Liam thinks to himself.

Upon arriving at the hospital, he wastes no time finding the room. He slowly opens the door to find both the women inside fast asleep. He quietly walks in, closing the door behind him, and tiptoes into the room. Not paying attention to where he is going, his foot hits the leg of a chair sitting against the wall. The loud screech of metal scrapping the floor awakes Raylene. She shifts in the chair, slowly at first. But seeing Liam standing in the dark shadows, she quickly stands as if looking for something to throw.

Liam realizes that she has no idea who he is. He swiftly walks into the light, "Raylene—it's me," he whispers.

The familiarity of his voice seems to calm her. She rushes over to him and throws her arms around his neck before Liam has time to say anything more.

"I'm so glad you are okay. I have been so worried about you."

She lets go of him, stands back, giving him a look that lets him know he is in trouble. The last time he saw that look was on his mom's face whenever he did something to upset her.

"Why haven't you been taking my calls? And where have you been?" she scolds at him, "your clothes are dirty and torn and you smell like dry mud." She snarls up her nose as she observes him. "Are you just going to stand there or are you going to explain yourself?"

He can't help but smile at how cute she looks with her hands on her hips, glaring up at him like a mad red hen with its feathers all ruffled.

"Do you think this is funny Liam? Because I don't. You have had me worried all da—"

"Raylene—can I speak now?" he grins down at her, fighting the urge to pull her into his arms and kiss those pouting lips. If only this were another time and place—under different circumstances—he wouldn't have to hold back.

"Sorry—but I have been worried about you." She motions for him to have a seat in the chair he just kicked.

He fills her in on where he has been all day and all the new information he now has on Trevor.

"I just can't get use to him being called Trevor—I still call him Kurt." She shakes her head before continuing, "That's the only name I ever knew him by—how can someone be so heartless as to take on his dead father's name?"

"Trevor—Kurt—is truly a unique person." It was the only thing he could think to say to this question, "but—in all this craziness of today, I have some good news."

"Well, you've already made it clear that you don't have my daughter—so, what other good news could you have?" she smiles as she anticipates his answer.

"Ronny is coming to Georgia."

"How is that good news for me?"

"Well—he has a traveling partner."

She responds only with a confused look as she waits for him to continue.

"Someone back in Chicago misses you—he refuses to eat and is constantly searching for you, so—"

"Dax? He's bringing Dax here?" her mom stirs in her sleep; Raylene places her finger over her lip; she hadn't meant to get so excited. Waiting to make sure Irene is going to stay asleep, she continues softly, "I can't believe I'm saying this—but I have missed him too. I never thought I could get so attached to a dog; I've never considered myself a dog person. But Dax has grown on me over the weeks I've had him."

"Well, it seems you have grown on him too. I spoke with River, she said he has never acted this way since he was placed in her care."

"When will he get here?"

"He's waiting to see when your mom will be going home. Most hotels frown on dogs staying in them. He thought it would be best if he could bring him straight to you."

"I can't wait to see him."

Liam sat and chatted for a few minutes more. He could talk to her all night, but noticing how tired she was getting, he decided to say his goodbyes and head back to her mom's house to sort through the new information and make some phone calls. It was going to be a long night— probably for both of them. He was starting to understand Dax's reactions to being away from her.

****

Liam sits out on the front steps of Irene's house as he awaits Raylene's arrival. He still can't believe the doctors are sending her home so soon. He guesses that Irene insisted she be sent home. But he can't blame her; he looks out over the fields that surround the property. She has a beautiful paradise to view as she recovers. So why would she want to stay in a dark, gloomy hospital room?

He realizes that he has never asked Raylene about her life before Trevor. But from the look of things, her dad must have been a farmer. Out by the old barn is a tractor, along with plows of different sorts, a baler, harrows, and a seed drill. It doesn't appear that any of the equipment has been used in a while. Remembering that Raylene had mentioned being a daddy's girl, he smiles as he imagines a much younger girl sitting up on the tractor with her dad.

The sun reflecting on a white object in the distance draws his eyes towards the windy road leading to the house. He watches as it comes closer. Then, standing, he smiles as he walks out to greet them. "I see you finally made it home," he says as he walks over to help Irene from the car.

"You know how hospitals are. It seems to take them forever to get someone released." Raylene walks around to assist.

Working together, they get Irene settled in for a nap. Just as they enter the living room, Liam smiles over to Raylene, "I'll be back in just a minute. I have to get something from outside." Not giving her a chance to speak, he heads through the kitchen and out the backdoor.

He had been so afraid the surprise would be ruined. But Dax had been a good dog and didn't make a sound when they arrived. Liam's guess was he was sleeping.

He opened the door to the barn slowly, and sure enough, there he was, curled up in a pile of hay, asleep. Hearing Liam's shuffling footsteps as he walks across the barn, Dax's head shoots up with a quiet, "woof." Then, seeing Liam, he jumps up and heads towards him, "Come on boy, I have a surprise for you."

As they walk back towards the house, Dax is right on Liam's heels. Raylene is standing in the backdoor; the two see each other at almost the same time. The dog snorts happily as he bonds forward. Then, running towards each other, she goes down on one knee to take the ecstatic dog in her arms as he leaps to her. "Dax, you're here!" she exclaims as the dog places sloppy kisses on her face.

"He seems happy to see you too." Liam laughs.

Raylene lets out a happy yelp as the weight of the wiggly dog pushes her to the ground. Liam watches the two of them, taking in the laughter coming from a woman that has been through so much over the past few months, and yet, an overweight golden retriever has given her joy.

"Don't just stand there smiling—help me!"

Taking Dax by the collar, "Come boy," he says as he gently pulls the dog back.

Raylene quickly jumps to her feet. "He's stronger than he looks," she laughs, brushing the leaves and dirt off her sweater. "I've got to go check on mom." She turns and walks back towards the house with the dog right on her heels.

Liam stops and fills a bowl with water, placing it on the floor for the dog; he enters the living room just as Raylene bonds down the stairs.

"I'm calling the hospital," she says as she reaches for the phone, "mom has a low-grade fever—I don't think that is a normal symptom with post-op."

Watching as she paces the floor, he listens contently to the conversation. She has a reason for concern; a fever could be a signal that something isn't right.

"I gave her Tylenol, yes—and if it continues or goes higher? Okay, thanks." She ends the call and runs her hand through her hair.

"He said to not be concerned at this point—just watch her." She takes a seat on the sofa and pulls her knees up to her chest, "I'm really scared of losing her. I wish they would let me bring her in to be checked."

Liam sits beside her, taking her hands in his, "We'll check her again in a little bit, and if her fever hasn't reduced will take her to the emergency room."

"Some days I feel as if my life is falling apart," she begins, as tears fill her eyes, "He takes my daughter; I was supposed to be her protector. Now, I don't even know where she is—don't know if she is being fed, bathed—nor do I know if she's safe," she exhales loudly, "I've failed her. What kind of mother—"

"Raylene, stop. You are not a bad mother. Don't let Trevor cause you to think this is all your fault."

"I'm not just a horrible mother—look what I let happen to my mom. What has she ever done to deserve this?"

"None of this is your fault. We are getting closer to having your daughter back with you and—"

"Are we?" Doubt drips from her words, "He seems to be a few feet ahead of us—every time, he seems to have the upper hand."

"That's what he wants you to think, Raylene—"

She holds up her hand to stop him, "How many other people have got to get hurt? Liam, I have tried to stay optimistic—but the truth is, he's winning." Her lip quivers as the tears turn into sobs. "I just want my daughter to come back to me. I pray every day that God will bring her home safely—but it's as if He isn't listening."

Liam pulls her into his arms as the sobs take over, "God is listening, Raylene—He will bring her home."

He held onto her as if the shelter of his arms could hold her together. After a while, the sobs stop. The shallow rise and fall of her breathing told him she had fallen asleep. A snort across the room told him Dax, too, is in dreamland. Liam had to smile despite the circumstances. Laying his head on top of Raylene's, he decides to let them sleep for a while.

An hour later, he awakes to what feels like pins pricking his fingers. Gently, he tries to maneuver his arm out from under the sleeping woman beside him. He hadn't meant to fall asleep. Liam freezes as Raylene stretches, hoping he has not awakened her. He watches as her eyelids blink open and closed a few times, and then he is staring into the green depths of her confused stare.

"Sorry, I was trying to not wake you. I wanted to check on your mom."

With the mention of Irene, she quickly rises from the sofa, "Oh goodness, why did you let me sleep?" she calls out as she runs up the stairs, not giving him a chance to respond.

Within a few minutes, they were on their way to the hospital. As he drives through the evening traffic, Liam keeps glancing up to the reflection of the women in the backseat. Worry is clearly etched on Raylene's face. Upon arriving at the emergency entrance, he notices the tremble in her hands as they assist Irene inside. He wanted to assure her everything was going to be okay. But he didn't want to make promises on something he wasn't sure of himself.

Minutes seem like hours, as he waits to hear news. All he has at times like this is his faith in God. So, he does all he knows to do—he prays. Not only does he pray that Irene will recover, but he also prays that Trevor will be apprehended, Nylah will be back with her mom, and that Raylene will have a happy ending to all this chaos. He rises and rushes to the door as Raylene walks inside.

"How is she—is she going to be alright?"

"She's stable. The nurses got her fever down. She is staying here to receive antibiotic drip. Because—" she wipes at a tear that has escaped her eye, "she has an infection that has spread into her blood stream, it's called sepsis." She takes a deep breath and blows it out slowly before continuing, "It can be fatal," she whispers through trembling lips.

"Hey," he says as he pulls her to him, "Don't think about the negative here, Raylene, God can and will bring her out of this—just keep praying and don't lose your faith in Him—not now when you need Him most."

"I can't Liam," she whispers between sobs.

"Can't what?"

"I can't pray—I always have and I did when all this first started. I prayed every day, every minute—but I don't understand why He is letting all this happen."

"Sometimes we don't understand things, Raylene. We just have to trust His *will* and know that He will get us through whatever that *will* may be."

"I'm trying to do that, Liam, I really am. However, right now, I feel He is punishing me. For what I don't know—but that's how I feel."

The nurse came in to lead them upstairs to ICU. Liam has never felt so helpless in his life. One thing he has learned in life—losing a close loved one has a way of testing your faith. But you can't ever lose that faith. Faith in God is all you have when you don't have anything else.

Chapter 13
Trevor

Sweat beads on his forehead and runs steadily down his face; Trevor wipes it away from his eyes using the back of his hand. As pain-induced nausea overtakes him, he squints as he searches the city streets for a safe place to stop for a while. He wouldn't be in this situation if his *wife* had acted the way she should. Why is she sitting there flirting with another man? You would think she would be upset with her family falling apart, but no, she's busy entertaining Mr. Detective.

He swerves into a parking spot by the curb, glances at the reflection of the scared little girl in the backseat. "I need you to be on your best behavior—you hear me?"

She nods in response.

"Hasn't your mama taught you the correct way to answer people? Answer me correctly." He demanded the child.

"Y-yes sir."

"And stop acting like you're scared of me—If I was going to hurt you, I would have already."

She started to nod but then whispered, "Yes sir."

Once on the sidewalk, he takes his daughter's hand and leads her to a bench in front of what looks like an old, abandoned store. "We'll sit her for a minute. I've got to find someone to look at this leg" He stretches out his leg, revealing a dark stain where the blood had dried; a crimson circle formed, indicating that the wound was bleeding again.

The drive from Blue Ridge to Gainesville had been rough. The pain was almost more than he could bear. If Brenda had been more understanding, he could have gone there. However, she probably would have called the cops before he ever got his car in park. He had hoped he could mend things between them, especially right now when he needs her most. And if not for him, then for her niece.

As pain courses through his leg, he looks up and down the sidewalk. This part of town looks deserted, void of any life at all. Across the street is an old, broken-down factory of some sort, so at some point, this part of town must have been a more exuberant place. He wouldn't be finding help here; that was obvious. The hospital is just a few streets over, but that would be like going to his sister's house. As soon as they put his name in the system, the cops would be there in a flash.

"Kurt," his daughter brings him out of his thoughts.

"Don't you know it's disrespectful to call your parents by their name?"

"Sorry." She replies meekly. "D-dad—I'm hungry."

He stares out at the old factory across the street as if it holds all the answers to his problems. He is running out of cash. Using his debit card would make him easy to track. However, he is out of options; either get money or starve. The car will be needing gas soon. With his leg wound, walking is out of the question. Driving is hard enough to do with the pain shooting through it.

Looking down into the big eyes staring up at him, he realizes that he hasn't answered her plea for food. "Me too. Look—there's a lot you don't know about me—m-my name isn't Kurt, it's Trevor. And you don't have to call me dad if you don't want to. I guess I haven't ever really acted like a daddy towards you, and—I-I'm sorry for that."

She doesn't respond, only turns to stare down at her hands as they lay on her lap.

Trevor jumps at the sound of the door opening to his left. He turns to look just as an older man walks out.

"Hello there." The man smiles at the open-mouth faces of Trevor and Nylah, "I saw the two of you sitting out here—didn't know if you needed some kind of assistance."

Trevor just looks at him blankly for a while before finally responding, "Sorry, I thought this area was deserted."

"For the most part it is. My wife and I bought this old store and we're renovating into a church." He turns to look up at the building, "Oh, by the way, my name is Steven McDuffie—and you are?"

"Kur—Trevor," he stands and extends his hand. "This is Nylah—my daughter."

"Nice to meet you, Trevor. What brings you to this side of town?"

"I'm not from here—I-We live in Chicago."

"I see," as he looks the two over his eyes rest on the bloodstain on Trevor's pant leg, "Seems you have an injury there."

"Yes," Trevor stalls as he searches for something to say, "I-I—we went hiking earlier today, I fell, and a stick punctured my leg."

"Why don't you come on in and let my wife have a look at it—it really looks bad."

"We couldn't be a bother. I'm sure it will be fine."

"We have an apartment above the store. Come on up. We'll get you fixed up, and—that little one looks like she could use a good, hot meal."

Trevor wants to turn him down, but with his daughter's pleading eyes staring up at him, saying no would mean having to get cash, and they both could use a hot meal. "Are you sure we wouldn't be a bother?"

"I'm sure of it. Come on in." Mr. McDuffie holds the door as they walked inside. Then, leads them through to the back of the building and up a flight of stairs.

As they walk into the living quarters of the upstairs apartment, it is like walking through a magic portal. It is delicately decorated, with a cozy feel about it. The smell of cornbread filling the air, giving it a homey feel.

"Wow, this is not what I expected." he says as he takes a seat on the big, oversized sofa.

"Clara did an outstanding job on the place, didn't she?" Steven McDuffie smiles at his wife lovingly as she enters the room.

"Oh, stop. You did more of the work than I did—I just told you what to do." She swats at her husband before turning to her guest. "I'm Clara, I've been married to this goof for almost fifty years." Her soft laugh speaks of a woman with a warm heart.

"Clara, this is Trevor and his daughter—" he looks to Trevor for the name.

"Nylah"

"What a lovely name for such a lovely young lady." She smiles down at the girl. "Dinner is almost ready. I hope you came hungry."

"Before we eat dear, do you mind taking a look at this young man's leg—seems he had an accident while hiking today."

Her eyes widen as she notices the bloody leg of Trevor's jeans. "I most certainly will. Let me get the first aid kit from the bathroom."

After Clara had him cleaned up, bandaged, and in a fresh pair of jeans that were just a little too big, Trevor sat down to the best hamburger vegetable soup he had eaten in a while. He listened to Steven's plans for the little store building, how God had sent him and his wife here to start a ministry. Nylah seemed to enjoy the attention she received from the older woman. He could tell she missed her mom. Knowing this touched a part of his heart that he was sure had numbed a long time ago.

He sits listening to the man talk, not really hearing the words he is saying. Yet, something in him was changing as he looked at the sad eyes of his daughter. Although she is smiling as Clara speaks, the smile doesn't quite register in her eyes. Not the way they used to when he watched her with her mom.

"The way that temperature is dropping—I think we just might get that snow they're calling for tonight." Steven reaches to turn the dial on the wall to adjust the heat.

"Snow?' Trevor's attention is suddenly back on the preacher. "It's supposed to snow tonight?" His mind starts to race; this means they will need a warm place to sleep tonight. But unfortunately, he doesn't have money for a hotel room. Which means he will have to go by the ATM to take out cash.

"Yeah, that's Georgia weather for you." Steven laughs.

"Nylah, dear, we need to be heading out if we want to make it home before it the snow starts." He smiles to his daughter, hoping she will play along.

"We're going home?" she exclaims with more joy and exuberance than he has seen since he took her that cold night in Chicago weeks ago.

"Sweetie, you help Ms. Clara with the dishes a little more—I want to talk to daddy a minute." Steven smiles up to his wife as he ushers the girl back to the kitchen.

"Trevor, I have something I want to share with you before you go." He took a seat on the sofa opposite him. "I don't know your story, and you don't have to tell me. But I know you are running from something. I see a sadness in you—confusion too. The moment I saw the two of you sitting outside this building, I knew God had sent you here. You have been running from God for a long time—haven't you?"

Trevor only nods.

"You don't have to run any longer. All you have to do is give it to Him and your life can be so much better. Only He can give you the peace that you are searching for."

"You don't understand. I—" Trevor takes a deep breath as he searches for the words to say. Words that won't tell that he is a wanted man on the run. "I have done some things that are very unforgivable. Not just this present situation—I turned away from God a very long time ago. I have done some very bad things."

"Son, we all have a past. I spent three years in prison when I was in my early twenties for fraud. In my thirties I spent two years on the inside for drug charges. I thought I was young and invincible. The turning point was when I was facing life in prison for a crime I did not commit. But because of my priors, it was hard to convince anyone that I didn't do it. I was mad at the world, and almost lost the best thing that ever happened to me—my wife. But I knew she was praying for me. So, one day I decided to go to church with her—just to shut her up. However, that was the day that changed my life forever. Just like you, I was convinced that I had done too many bad things for God to forgive me. I was wrong, and you are too."

Trevor brushed at the tears that were streaming down his face. "I want to do what's right." He whispered.

"Do you want to pray?"

Trevor nodded yes.

After finishing the prayer, he took down the preacher's phone number and address. The snow was already starting to fall as they left the McDuffie's. But his only thought was on righting the wrongs he has done. He's going back to Blue Ridge; once there, he is taking his daughter back to her mama and turn himself in. He knows this will mean that he will spend the rest of his life in prison. But he has a newfound peace that tells him everything will work out fine.

Snow lashes against the windshield of his car as he drives down a deserted, one-lane road. The roads leading into Blue Ridge are curvy and mountainous. Lost in thought, he doesn't realize that he is going a little over the speed limit. His tires slip a little on the wet, slushy pavement, but he manages to keep the car steady. He peers through the front window, trying to see what is ahead of him; it is pitch black outside, with not even one star in the night sky. Outside the front window, the snow is coming down in torrents, blurring Trevor's vision even more. The windshield wipers whip back and forth over the window, doing little to clear away the fluffy flakes clinging to the glass.

Looking out his side window, Trevor is a little uneasy as he notices that all he can see is blackness, speckled with white dots of snow. Two blinding lights suddenly blaze ahead like two shining eyes trying to pierce the impenetrable darkness—with a jolt, Trevor realizes that those lights belong to a car—a car speeding towards him from the opposite direction—but in his lane. Again, Trevor takes in the wall of darkness around him— he has no idea what is hidden in its blackness. It could be a wall of trees or a mountain overlook with an almost endless bottom.

He slams on his brakes and turns the car so that the passenger's side is to the oncoming vehicle. The sound of screeching brakes and tires skidding on the wet, slushy pavement shattered the immense silence that had been pressing in on Trevor all night. Suddenly, his car spins out of control towards the oncoming vehicle; images flash across his mind—images of Raylene and clips of his life flashing past like a slideshow that has been sped up.

A huge blow hits the car, and it seems like a tremendous weight is thrown on Trevor; the last thing he sees is a waterfall of glass cascading down on him before everything goes black, and the immense weight lifts off him as he seems to float into complete and utter darkness.

Chapter 14
River

Looking at her watch for the fifth time, River wondered what could be keeping Liam. He was supposed to meet her here an hour ago. Several attempts to reach him on his cellphone had been unresponsive. She pulls her thin blazer tighter around her. After last night's snowstorm, the temperature had dropped to degrees lower than it should be in Georgia this time of year. Upon deciding it is too cold to wait any longer outside, she walks through the automatic doors into the emergency room waiting area.

Raylene is probably concerned about their arrival. The thought of conducting business meetings in situations like this makes River uncomfortable. Raylene is dealing with a lot right now. This infection in Irene's blood is getting better, but she still has a long road ahead of her before she's truly out of danger. All anyone can do at this point is pray that God spares her; sepsis can be very deadly.

She takes a seat in view of the doors. Hopefully, Liam will be here soon. Looking around the room, she spots a little girl sitting behind the nurse's station. The blanket wrapped around her seems to do little to warm the girl. Her face is streaked with tear stains. River can't help but wonder why she is here. The fear in the little girl's eyes breaks her heart. Unable to stand it any longer, she walks over to the desk.

"Hi, I know it's none of my business," she begins while flashing her badge to the nurse, hoping it will get her some information, "What's the deal here?"

The receptionist glances at the girl, then leaning towards River, she whispers, "She was in an accident a little while ago, it was just her and her dad. He's in surgery—not doing too well."

"Where's her mom?"

"We don't know. She's not saying anything, and the dad was unresponsive when they arrived. No identification has been made yet."

"That's sad—poor kid."

"There you are."

At the sound of her partner's voice, she turns around.

"It's about time—where have you been?"

She smiles to the nurse before joining Liam, "I hope they find her family soon," she says as they walk towards the elevator.

"I'm sorry, apparently there was a bad accident out on 76. Traffic was at a standstill for an hour."

"Really?" she says as she points behind her, "I wonder if it was the same accident that little girl was involved in?"

Liam only shrugs.

River exhales loudly as they reach Irene's door. "I really hate doing this here, but we have to ask her more questions—we have nothing else to go on at this point."

They quietly walk through the door. Raylene looks up and straightens in her chair as they enter the room.

"Hey, I thought you guys had decided to not come." She smiles at them.

"We would never abandon our favorite client," Liam interjects as he walks into the room.

"No, but apparently, we can make them wait," River jokingly points to her partner.

"Hey—it wasn't my fault."

"That's his story. However true it may be—we'll never know."

Raylene smiles to the two of them as she stands to greet them.

"I was thinking we'd have this chat in the cafeteria. I can use some coffee." She walks past them towards the door, "I've got to get out of this room for a while."

"Sounds like a good idea. I could use a cup too. Especially after standing outside for an hour waiting for a certain person."

Liam chuckles as they walk out into the hallway.

The three of them engage in small talk and jabs as they make their way to the cafeteria. River chooses a table in the far corner, and Liam goes to retrieve coffee for them. "I'm sorry to have to do this here." She says to Raylene as they have a seat.

"It's okay. I'm so desperate for a distraction from this hospital right now." She smiles to the detective. "But, more than that—I want to find my daughter."

Liam joins them and places steaming cups in front of them.

"I'm just going to be straight with you," River began, "we are all out of leads—we have nothing. I know that is not what you want to hear right now; but we are nowhere close to finding Trevor than we were when we thought he was Kurt. With all the new information, you'd think we'd have something. But—" she looks to Liam to take over.

"Raylene, we need you to think really hard right now—is there anyone you can think of that might know where he could be hiding? We have every motel and hotel in this area and in Chicago on the lookout for a man traveling with a little girl. So, we know he's not staying at those. He's hurt—he hasn't been to any hospitals—but he's had to get help from somewhere."

"Trevor has always been a private person. I didn't even know he had a sister. Like I've already told you—he never spoke of family, even got mad if I mentioned it. All I know about him is what I've learned during all this." She pauses as emotions begin to take over, "What about the couple—what's their names? Wyatt and Sarah?"

"That's part of what me and Ronny have been working on." River says.

"And?"

153

"We've been following them and even tried talking with them again. Apparently, Trevor isn't contacting them anymore. Wyatt is upset because he hasn't got paid lately."

"So, if they did know of his whereabouts, they would give him up." Liam interjected.

Raylene went back through the small list of people that her husband had dealt with through the years. The ones that she knew of anyway. River can see the fear of defeat flash in the woman's eyes.

"Don't lose hope Raylene—we're going to find him."

"I know you will. It's just killing me not knowing if my daughter is being taken care of properly." she glances at her cellphone to check the time, "I've got to get back upstairs. Mom will be waking up soon."

Liam is the first to stand, "If it's alright, I'm going to head over and check on Dax."

"I will see Raylene back upstairs, and I will check in with Ronny to see if anything has happened since he arrived back in Chicago."

"Sounds like a good plan to me." Liam says his goodbyes as he walks away.

River continues to assure Raylene that they will work endlessly to find Nylah. She wishes there was more she could say to give her hope. This has to be a mother's worst nightmare come true. Before her husband's death, they had talked endlessly about having kids someday. However, they never got the chance before he was suddenly taken from her. But her instincts told her that this woman was dying inside without her child. As they walk past the gift shop, a teddy bear in the window display catches River's eye. Her mind drifts back to the little girl in the emergency room.

"I'm sorry—but I want to buy this teddy for the little girl in the ER. She was in an accident and her dad is not doing too well, I think she could use a friend while they locate her family."

"Sure, I'm going to stop by the lady's room while you do that." Raylene calls out as River enters the shop.

River walks once again to the desk, "I have a little friend looking for someone special to hang out with." She says to the lady as she nods towards the little girl.

The receptionist smiles as she takes the teddy bear and hands it to the child.

River notices that she has stopped crying. But the look of fear is still in her eyes. "Have you located her family yet?"

"No, social services are trying to find somewhere for her to stay until—" her words drift off. "It's not looking too good for her daddy." She whispers.

"I hope things turn out good for him." She replies.

She walks back out into the hallway just as Raylene exits the bathroom. "My heart aches for that little one." She says to her as they head up the hallway towards the elevator.

"I know she has to be scared. I often wonder if Nylah feels the same way—being away from me and all. Me and that little girl have something in common—she longs to be back with her mom—I long to be back with my daughter."

River stops walking, "You know what? You just gave me an idea—I'm going to call social services and see if I can take her home with me—until they find her family."

"I think you should."

"Do you want to go back with me and meet her?"

"I need to get back to mom—sorry."

River rushes back to the ER to share her news. She hopes that social services will allow her to keep the girl. It would be better than her sitting behind the nurse's station alone. A smile stretches across the receptionist's face as she tells her the news.

"Social Services will be happy to hear this. They asked me about taking her—I would, but I have no room for her."

After a phone call and a dozen papers signed later, River walks out into the cold Georgia air hand in hand as she leads the child to her car. Their first stop would be to buy her some clothes. Maybe once she had the bloody evidence of the accident washed away, she could get some information out of her. She looks the child over as she buckles her into the car. For some reason, she seems so familiar. Maybe she has seen her around somewhere, but it's hard to tell with the bruises and butterfly bandages that hold together her wounds.

She walks around the car and buckles herself in the driver's seat, "My name is River, I'm going to let you stay at my house until we can find your mommy, okay?"

The little girl only nods.

"Can you tell me your name—just so I know what to call you."

The girl stares at her hands in silence, and River doesn't want to pressure her, so they continue to the shopping strip near the hospital. "You don't have to tell me your name if you don't want to. But, how about we think of something for me to call you—okay?"

She pulls into the parking lot and parks her car, "We're going to stop and get you some new clothes, you like shopping?" she enquires the little girl as she helps her from the car.

The little girl nods yes.

"Okay then, we'll call you---Shoppy." She is relieved when the girl smiles and shakes her head no.

"You don't like Shoppy?" again she smiles and shakes her head, "Well, let me think—humm—what about Happy?" she enquires as she pushes a shopping cart into the store.

This time the little girl giggles, "Noo," she says.

River is amazed at how the girl seems to be warming up to her. "Then what can I call you?" she smiles down to her.

"Nylah." The little girl replies.

River stops in her tracks. A warm tingle floods over her as she wonders if she just heard the little girl right. "What did you just say? Did you say Nylah?"

River tries to keep the shock out of her voice. Could it be? Could this little girl be Raylene's daughter? She watches as the girl nods yes. Then, trying hard not to alarm the child, she grabs the first outfit she comes to in her size. She must get home and call Liam. She can't wait to tell him that she may have fortuitously found Raylene's daughter.

Chapter 15
Liam

The car skids to a stop as Liam pulls in front of River's apartment complex. He swiftly exits the car. Then bounds across the sidewalk and approaches the building; he swings open the door and takes the stairs two at a time to the second floor. He takes a minute to calm himself before ringing her doorbell.

His thoughts are racing as he waits for her to answer. Could Raylene's daughter really be on the other side of this door? Everything about this case has been ironic, or was it just a coincidence? In the beginning, he and River had been summoned to Chicago to investigate a crooked cop. Then was asked to look into the case of a woman who had shown up at a convenience store stabbed. Only to find out that the woman was the wife of the cop they were investigating.

Ultimately, they end up back in Georgia. Unfortunately, the woman's mother gets shot by the daughter's husband. An infection causes her to return to the hospital on the same day a little girl shows up abandoned by an accident. His partner decides to take in that little girl while her family is located because her father may not survive his injuries. It all sounds a little confusing, yet Liam was eager to get to the bottom of this and hopefully return Raylene's daughter.

As River opens the door, he quietly slips inside. "Where is she?"

"She in the bath. How are we going to approach this?"

"We'll show her the picture of Raylene and see how she responds."

"I have coffee made if you want to help yourself while I go get her from the bath."

Liam takes a cup from the shelf above the coffee pot and fills it with the black liquid. He leans against the counter as he sips slowly from the cup. What is taking her so long? It can't be that difficult to remove a child from the tub and get her dressed. His anxiety is about to get the best of him when he finally hears them coming from the hallway.

"I was about to come looking for you." He says to River, then smiles to the little girl, "Hi, you must be Nylah."

She shyly grasps onto the leg of River's slacks and ducks behind her.

"You don't have to hide, baby girl. This is my friend Liam. He's here to help us find your mommy." She takes the little girl by the hand and leads her forward. "He has a picture he wants you to look at and tell us if it's a picture of your mom, okay?"

She nods sheepishly.

Liam walks to the table and picks up the file folder he had brought with him. Opening it, he takes out the picture of Raylene and shows it to the girl.

"Mommy!" she exclaims as she grabs the picture from his hand.

River and Liam exchange looks of relief as River kneels in front of the little girl, "What if I told you that we know where your mommy is?"

Nylah looks up from the picture and stares hopefully at River.

"Do you want to go see her?"

She nods and turns to walk towards the door.

"I'll drive." Liam offers, and the three of them head towards the stairwell.

"Should we call her or just show up?" River enquires.

"Just show up. I want this to be a surprise."

The short drive to the hospital seems to take forever. Even the elevators seem slower than usual. As they approach the door, they pause. They haven't planned on how this is going to happen. Liam looks to River, "So—do we just barge in?"

"No—you go in ahead of us. We'll wait out here while you fill her in. Just let me know when you are ready for us to join you."

Nylah has been quiet ever since getting the news. She looks up to River as Liam walks through the door and closes it in front of them. Liam knows she is anxious to be with her mom. He slips quietly inside the room. Raylene looks up from a book she is reading as she hears the door open.

"Hi," she says as she lays the book on the bedside table, "I'm so happy you're here. Mom just got some good news."

"Really?" Liam asks.

"She gets to go home tomorrow."

"That's great!" Liam pulls a chair close to her and sits down, "I have some good news too. Remember the little girl that River took in earlier today?"

Raylene nods. Then her eyes light up as a big smile spread across her face, "Oh! Did they locate her family? Is that the good news—I have had her on my mind all day—I bet she is thrilled to be back with them—"

"Raylene, no." he pauses as he searches for the best way to tell her, "River finally got her to talk—her name is Nylah." He explores her face for a response. Nothing.

"Did you hear what I just said?"

"Yes. I was just thinking that it's ironic."

"What is?"

"Even though I've never met this little girl—I felt a connection with her—like, we have something in common. And now you tell me that she shares the same name as my daughter."

"Yeah," Liam nods as he tries to hold back the smile that is trying to break through, "It's because she is your daughter."

There was a short pause, and then he watches as recognition beams in her eyes.

"What did you say? Liam, don't play with me." She cups her hands over her mouth, "You have Nylah? Where is she?" she stands and looks past him.

"She's here—just on the other side of that door." He looks over his shoulder, "River." He calls out.

The door opens slowly. He watches the reactions of mother and child as their eyes meet for the first time in months.

"Nylah! Oh, my baby!" Raylene exclaims as she scoops the child up in her arms.

"Mommy! Mommy!" he watches as tears stream down both their faces.

Glancing behind the mother and child, he makes eye contact with River. She, too, has tears streaming down her face. Not much different than himself. He clears his throat and quickly brushes the tears away. River gives him a knowing smile. In the years they have been working together, this is the first time he has ever shown his emotions in front of her.

Raylene lovingly wipes her daughter's face with the sleeve of her shirt. After a while, she turns to Liam, "So, what about Kurt? Is he going to be alright?"

"Mommy," Nylah interrupts, "he told me his name is not Kurt. It's Trevor."

"Yes, my love, that is true." She looks to Liam for support. Her look told him she wasn't sure how much to tell her daughter.

"From what I'm being told, he's—" he searches for a way to continue in front of a child.

"It's okay. Go on." Raylene urges him.

"—not too good. To put it short, he has many broken bones and some internal bleeding. They are keeping him in a drug-induced coma for now."

A shuffle from the bed made everyone turn towards Irene.

"What did I miss?" she asks as she pushes herself up in bed. "Why is everyone crying?"

Raylene pulls her daughter close, "Nylah, I have someone I want you to meet."

"Did you just say Nylah?" Irene sits straighter as she peers at Raylene. "Is this—has she—oh my!" Irene stutters as she tries to contain herself.

"Yes! Nylah, this is your grandma—mom this is Nylah."

Liam watches as the two women beam with joy. It's cases like this that make his job worthwhile—even if they do get solved by chance.

Chapter 16
Raylene

The lights from the monitors cast an eerie glow across Trevor's face as Raylene sits in the darkness staring at the man she has been married to all these years. With all the bruises and tubes, it's hard to tell it's really him. Yet, she can't help but wonder how he would look to her even without them. So much has changed over the course of a few short months.

She knew he had secrets, but never in her life would she have thought that those secrets were what they turned out to be. Who is this man in front of her? He is but a stranger now. If he woke up, what would she say to him? She misses the man she first met. He was so loving and compassionate. Was that part a lie too? Was it all lies?

Raylene remembers the way they used to laugh. Those memories run through her mind now like a movie. Meeting him at the end of her dad's life had seemed like an answered prayer. Her daddy was her life. The man she looked up to and adored. *Kurt* had taken her mind off the pain of losing him. She was so convinced of the love between them that she left her mom behind to start a new life in Chicago.

Of course, she didn't know that it would be nine years before she would be allowed to see her mom again. She had envisioned vacations to Georgia or her mom visiting Chicago. Especially as the babies came along, she had imagined her mom coming on extended visits to help during those first weeks. Instead, Irene was denied four years of her granddaughter's life. Tears fill her eyes as she thinks of her daughter.

Raylene had always wanted a big family. Being an only child, she had always wanted a brother or sister. Irene had explained that there would be no more babies. Raylene, herself, almost didn't make it here alive. Wiping the tears from her mom's eyes, she had promised her that one day she would give her many grandbabies. Look how that turned out.

This man, lying in front of her, has taken so much from her. And yet, here she sits in the dark, praying for God to spare his life. Everyone deserves a second chance. Or third. She's not really sure what number Kurt would be on. That's who he would always be to her—Kurt. Saying Trevor just doesn't feel right to her.

The light from the hallway fills the room as a nurse opens the door. Raylene rises from the chair as she enters. "I'm sorry, I was just leaving." She says as she walks towards the door.

"It's okay. You don't have to leave on my account."

Raylene gasps as she recognizes the person who walks in. "Brenda, hi—I thought you were the nurses coming in."

"I know it's early. I just couldn't get back to sleep after the detective called me—I tried to stay away—but here I am."

Raylene gives a weak smile to the woman. "Me too."

"I like to think that somewhere inside—the real Trevor is still there. He used to be such a loving and kind person."

"I think he is—I saw that side of him once too." She says as she heads for the door. "I've got to get back to mom. She'll be going home soon."

She closes the door behind her as she leaves. Brenda is a reminder that she is not the only person Trevor has hurt.

****

Raylene sits on the sofa, smiling over a hot cup of coffee, as she watches her daughter playing with Dax on the floor by the fireplace. She hasn't been able to take her eyes off her since River dropped her off an hour ago. Although Irene is almost immobile, she has still been playing the doting grandma so well. Hanging around here would surely result in a very spoiled little girl.

Nylah looks up from Dax, "Mom, ask Grammy if we can take him home with us."

"He doesn't belong to Grammy." She says with a smile. "I adopted him—that means he belongs to you and me." She points to herself and then to her daughter.

Nylah lets out a cheer as she hugs the oversized dog.

"Nylah? What do you think about moving here?"

"With Grammy?"

Raylene nods as she stands to answer the doorbell. "Yes, with Grammy."

"Yes!" she screams joyfully to Raylene's back.

"Come in." she says to Liam as she opens the door. Then in a whisper, "I haven't told her yet that I've got to leave—so give me a minute."

She walks to the door of the living room, "I've got to go check on K-Trevor. I want you to stay here and keep an eye on Grammy and Dax for me—can you do that?"

"Yay! Yes, I can."

"I don't know. Humm—that's a job for a big girl. Are you sure you can do a big girl's job?" she teases.

"I's a big girl, mommy."

"Okay, I'll be back shortly." She kisses her daughter on the cheek then turns to leave.

Not much is said as they make their way to the hospital. Traffic is light, so it takes no time at all to get there. As they approach Trevor's door, Liam stops at the waiting area and takes a seat.

"What are you doing?" Raylene peers down at him, confused.

"I'm going to wait here. He asked to speak with you—not me." He stands and takes her hand in his, "You got this—and I'm right here if you need me."

She had been nervous ever since she got the phone call that Trevor was awake and asking for her. To some, it may seem weird that she was on edge about talking to a man she had been married to for almost nine years, but it was as if she was going to see a stranger. She fights the urge to take hold of Liam's hand and drag him in there with her. However, she finally let go and walks the few steps to Trevor's door.

Opening it slowly, she walks inside. The gruesome sight of him sitting, propped up, was hard enough on her senses. But the way his lips are swollen from the tubes almost gave his smile an evil semblance. She shudders as she walks up to the chair sitting by the bed.

"I'm glad you came." He whispers. "I was—afraid—you wouldn't—come."

She only responds with a smile. The doctor had already advised her on his speech. A chalkboard lay on the bed beside him—just encase speaking became too much for him. Raylene took in the wires attached to his arms and hands and wondered how writing would be possible at all for him.

"How—is Nylah?"

"Kurt—" she shakes her head, "Trevor, I'm not here to make small talk. The doctor says it's not good for you to talk—please get to the point." She fights hard to keep the anger out of her voice, but it's a task she's failing.

"I know—I hurt you. I'm—sorry for—that." He begins as she sits there quietly. "I met—a preacher—before—" he motions to his injuries, "I—asked God—to for—give me—for my—sins."

"That's good—good for you." She motions for him to continue.

"I was—on—my way—to make—things right—and—to bring—Nylah—back to you." Once again, he points to himself, "Then this."

Raylene slides to the edge of her chair, "I want to believe you, Trevor, I really do. But how am I supposed to know what *your* truth is anymore?" The tears she has been trying to hold escape down her face, "It's like I never really knew you."

"I know—and—I'm sorry." She watches as tears well in his eyes, "I know—that's not—enough—to repay—but it's—all I—have."

Rising from the chair, she lays her hand on his, "Like I said, I want to believe you. However, right now—I can't. We'll talk more when you are better."

As she turns to walk away, he calls out to her again, "Raylene—I do—love you—I al-ways—have. If you—believe nothing-else—I've told you—believe that—please."

No words would come to respond to him. Instead, she only smiles and walks out the door. Then, seeing Liam stand as she approaches him, she runs into his arms and sobs. At this moment, she doesn't care who is watching. Liam had become her safety net, and right now, she needs the confinement of that safety.

Silence fills the car on the drive back to Irene's. Raylene knows if she tries to speak, the emotional flood gates will open again. But, then again, what is she going to say? Talking about her feelings at the moment may come across as heartless. There was a time when she deeply loved her husband. She had tried everything to make it work. However, it seemed that as she tried to bend to what he wanted, his wants changed. Nothing was ever good enough for him.

If she let her hair grow out, he wanted it short. Then, after cutting it, he made fun of her. He even told her once that no matter what she did, she would never be attractive. For the past nine years, she has let him call the shots on everything. But it was she who was belittled when he decided that wasn't what he wanted anymore.

Little by little, the love she once had for him started to die. With every passing day, she only went through the motions of what he had wanted at that moment. Jumping through hoops to make him happy until she had lost all sense of herself and who she really was. Who is she? What does she want?

When she had decided to tell Trevor that she was leaving, those questions prompted that decision. Nothing has changed. No matter how much he declares he's a changed man—she's not going back. He's done this before. How many times has he sworn that he was changing? And yet—here we are—at another one of those crossroads where he feels threatened, and what is he doing?

For his sake, she prays he is telling the truth. Everything in her wants to believe he has accepted God into his life. She has prayed for so long for that one thing. God is what has got her through these rough years with him. That was the one thing Trevor couldn't take from her—although he tried.

As Liam pulls up in front of her mom's house, he takes her hand in his, "God will work it all out, Raylene."

"I know," she whispers, "I just feel like I'm being unfair to him."

"In what way?"

"Liam, I can't pretend to feel something I don't—not anymore." She lays her head back on the headrest,

"The love I had for him died a while ago—I just can't pretend anymore."

"You don't have to, Raylene." He turns in his seat to face her, "*He* did this to himself—action have consequences—so don't feel guilty for the way you feel."

"I care about him, and I wish the best for him, but—I can't go back."

"Then don't."

She brushes the tears from her face and reaches for the door handle, "I've got to get back to Nylah," she smiles over to him, "Do you know how good it feels to say that?"

"I do," he returns her smile, "Now go spend time with that little girl—and get some rest."

She exits the car and heads into the house. Although sleep would be good right now, she will probably spend the night just staring at her daughter. It is so good to have her home again. Sleep will have to wait.

Chapter 17
Raylene

Throwing the covers back as she comes awake, Raylene rubs her eyes and checks the time. Who would be ringing a doorbell at this hour of the morning? She stumbles down the stairs and reaches the landing just as a *ding* sounds again, "I'm coming!" she yells to whoever is on the other side of the door. *This better be important*, she mumbles to herself as she yanks open the door.

"Liam? what on earth are you doing here this early?" she squints her eyes against the sunlight that is starting to slip through the tree branches. "Come in, it's cold."

"Good-morning to you too." He gives her a sarcastic smile, "You look—um—tired—for someone who just woke up."

"If my looks mattered, then you should have called ahead to tell me you were coming." She returns with the same smile.

"Is Nylah still sleeping?"

"Yess—you came here this early to visit Nylah?"

"No." Then turning more serious, "I need to—I have to tell you—" he can't seem to get the word to come.

"What?"

"We may need to have a seat for this." He motions towards the sofa. After they are settled, he continues. "I just got a call from the hospital."

"Okay, go on."

"Trevor—Trevor—Raylene, Trevor passed away last night."

"What?" She cups her hands over her mouth, "That can't be. He seemed fine when I left. Well—not fine, but he was talking to me—oh Liam, No. Even though, I was planning on asking for a divorce once all this is over—I didn't want anything bad to happen to him."

"Why do you say that as if his death is your fault?"

"The last thing I said to him was that I didn't believe he has changed. I could have been nicer—I could have said we'd talk about it later—"

Raylene, what does all that have to do with his passing? Nothing." He answers for her.

"Nylah—what am I going to tell her?" she does nothing to stop the tears from flowing down her face, "Have you told Brenda?"

"River is on her way there now."

"She wanted so badly to have her brother back—the way he once was."

"I know, I know." He shakes his head sadly. "Nylah will be waking up soon. Why don't you go get a shower and try to get your emotions under control—I'll cook up some pancakes and put on coffee."

Raylene nods her head in agreement, "That sounds great. You're right, I need to calm down before I have to talk with her." She turns to head towards the stairs, "Shouldn't we be going to the hospital?"

"No, the funeral home will call when they are ready for you to make arrangements—unless you want to go to the hospital?"

She stood there a few seconds, thinking. "No, it will be better this way." She turns and strolls up the stairs.

Once in her bathroom, she goes through the motions of showering and getting dressed. As she stares at her reflection in the mirror, her thoughts run wild. This was not the news she had wanted to hear today. Nylah has been back with her for less than twenty-four hours, and now she must go downstairs and tell her that her daddy is dead. Will she even care? It's not like he has ever been a daddy to her. But then again, what kind of bond, if any, did they create over these months that he had her.

The sound of the doorbell disrupts her thoughts. *God, please, no more bad news today,* she whispers as she heads back downstairs. Liam hands her a cup of coffee as she enters the kitchen, "Something smells delicious in here," she says as she takes the cup from him. "Although, I hope you are not upset if I'm unable to eat any of it."

"Under the circumstances—I might can let you slide." He gives her a warm smile.

"Oh, was that the doorbell I heard a minute ago?"

"Yes, an officer brought over Trevor's belongings from the hospital." He points to a bag sitting on the counter.

Raylene slowly opens the bag and removes the few items inside—his watch, wedding band, and wallet—and an envelope with her name on it. Her hands begin to shake as she rips open the seal. She reads the words to herself,

My Dearest Raylene,

I asked this kind nurse to pen these words for me. If you are reading this, then I have crossed to the other side. I want you to know that my love for you has always been true. I'm just sorry that I messed things up. Would you please tell Nylah I am sorry I've never been a daddy to her? She is an incredible little girl; you have done a great job with her so far. Please forgive me for all the things I put you through. You deserve so much more than I ever gave you. You are beautiful inside and out, and I know you will have no problem finding a man that can love you the way you should be loved. Don't let how I treated you keep you away from letting him in when he shows up. You deserve the best.

Love Always,

Trevor

PS.

There is a business card in my wallet with the name Steven McDuffie on it. Call him to speak at my funeral. And tell him I said 'thank you' for sharing Christ with me.

She folds the letter and shoves it back into the envelope. Feeling a little uncomfortable, she opens his wallet to find the card. She was surprised to see a picture of her and Nylah smiling up at her. When did he get this? She hadn't noticed any of her photographs missing. It was one that Mrs. Johnson had taken of them by the rose bushes. She takes out the business card and places the wallet back in the bag along with his other belongings.

"This is who he wants to speak over his—" she lets the words trail off.

"Is that what that letter was about?" he asks as he takes the card from her, "Steven McDuffie—I know this guy. He's a good man. I ran into him and his wife about a week ago while dining out."

"I wonder how Trevor knows him—not really the type he'd be hanging around—ya know." As she spoke, she remembered what Trevor had told her last night, "I wonder if he's the preacher he mentioned?"

"Do you want me to call him?"

"No—I think I will," she takes the card from him and shoves it in her pocket, "But later—right now I want to see how many of these pancakes I can eat."

****

The last few days have seemed surreal—she had been at the wake the night before. Now standing in the graveyard, staring at the closed casket sitting over a green blanket of what feels like plastic under her feet—she still can't believe this is happening. Even though she can't see him—Trevor is the one inside that gray and black box.

Raylene doesn't hear a word that Reverend McDuffie is saying. Instead, she is thinking about how much her life is changing. After nine years of abuse—it all ends like this? One moment she is telling him she's leaving, then a few months later, she's standing at his graveside. This is not the way it was supposed to end.

She holds tightly to Nylah's hand as she wonders what to do beyond this day. There were so many decisions to be made. Glancing around at the few people gathered to pay their respects, she wonders if they pity her or think she is a horrible person. After all, it has been three days since her husband's death, and she hasn't yet shed a tear. Not because of the indifference between them—she's just—numb. That's the only word that comes to mind that describes how she is feeling. Sadness clutches at her inner soul, and her heart bleeds a river inside—but yet her eyes are dry.

Reverend McDuffie jars her out of her thoughts as he gently places his hand on her shoulder, "I'm so sorry for your loss," he says with much compassion.

"Thank you." Her words are barely audible.

How could she say anything more? Would the preacher understand if he knew she had planned to leave him? Although, there is something in the way he looks at her that causes her to think that he understands. She looks around to find that most everyone has started towards their vehicles. Tugging at Nylah's hand, she begins to her own.

She sees an outline of a man propped up by a big oak tree. As they walk closer, the man straightens and heads towards them.

"Hiya?" Liam began, "How are you two holding up?"

Nylah only smiles up at him.

"We are going to be okay," Raylene gave a weak smile.

He walks with them to her car and waits as she buckles Nylah into the safety seat and closes the car door.

"How about you and Nylah joining me in a night of fun at the spring fair tomorrow night? I think it will help get your minds off all—this for a while." He waves his hand towards the gravesite.

"Liam—I'm not trying to sound mean, so please don't take it that I am," she looks around nervously, "But—your job is finished now. So, let's just all move along with our lives and not complicate things—okay?"

"I-I didn't mean it as a date—r-really—I just thought getting out would do the two of you some good. Just as friends—I thought—we were friends."

"I can't Liam. I need time to sort out my—" she looks back towards the grave, "I've got to figure out a lot of things right now. So, please, just go on with your life, because it will take a while for me to figure out mine— and Nylah's. good-bye."

She gets into the car and drives off, leaving him standing there. And for the first time in three days—she cries.

Chapter 18
Liam-One Year Later

Liam checks the gauges on the dashboard as he tries once again to start the car. Why is this happening now—at this moment? He can look under the hood, but that would do him no good. When it comes to cars, about all he knows is how to start them and go. The only thing he knows how to do is change a tire. But unfortunately, the tires have nothing to do with the engine starting.

He opens the door to make sure it is safely out of the traffic, then punches in River's number on his cell. She picks up almost immediately. "Hey, I need your help—no, car trouble—just past the third traffic light from the office—try to hurry, I'm calling a tow truck—thanks."

After calling the tow service, he tries once again to start the car—still nothing. This car would have to fail him on a day that he's already running late. Isn't that the way it always goes? He can't complain; he has been driving it for fifteen years. But it could have waited until tomorrow.

Breaking down on such an important day is not what he needs right now.

River and the tow truck pull up at almost the same time. Liam instructs the driver and pays him. Then, he hurriedly gets in the passenger seat of River's Toyota, "To my place—fast."

"Hey! Don't boss me—I'm saving you," she laughs.

"Saving me? Really?" he jokes back to his partner, "Is that the way you see this?"

"Not changing the subject, but how did things go with Raylene yesterday?"

"The house in Chicago is sold!" He throws his fist in the air in triumph.

"Oh, good! It's been what? About a year?"

"One year and three weeks since she put it on the market."

"How is Nylah adjusting? Any problems since— you know?"

"Raylene said that she hasn't had a nightmare in five months—so I think she's getting there—things like that take some time to get over—if ever."

"Especially for a child. That had to be scary for her."

Liam only nods. He recalls the day of the funeral. Hearing Raylene tell him she didn't need him around anymore had all but ripped his heart out. He knew she would need a friend, and yet she had pushed him away. But he had given her what she asked for. He had stayed away and didn't call. It took every ounce of strength he had not to at least dial her number.

About a month after the funeral service, she had called to ask a favor—she needed a good lawyer and thought that he might know someone that could help her. The insurance company had gotten hold of the information on the false identity, and therefore refused payment, stating that the policy was void because of this. Upon seeing that Raylene had lawyered-up, they decided that the policy wasn't invalid after all. Once again, Raylene went silent.

Just when he thought she had all but forgotten him, she calls for another favor. This time he was informed that the house in Chicago had been put on the market, and she needed to remove her belongings. He had been more than happy to help gather up a crew of strong men—along with himself—to assist with emptying the house. However, the buyers backed out.

Thinking back now, he's happy that the first sale didn't go through, because he has spent the remainder of this past year helping her bridge the gap with the agency. By the time they found a buyer, a true friendship had blossomed.

"You're home," River's words cut through his thoughts, "Unless you want to just sit there and stare out into space."

"Sorry, I was kinda caught up in reminiscing." He laughs as he reaches for the door handle.

"Well, you are going to be late if you don't get a move on," she pushes him towards the door, "Oh, do you think your truck will start?"

"Of course, why wouldn't it?"

"Maybe because it is as old as the vehicle that just left you stranded."

"You just love giving me a hard time, don't you?" he laughs as he steps from the car, "I have a rental being delivered. So, it wouldn't matter anyway."

"Ah, so you didn't trust the truck." She jokingly points at him, "Hey Liam—don't be nervous—you got this," she adds on a more serious note.

"Thanks, you're such a good friend to have around."

"I feel more like your mother most days."

They both laugh as he closes the car door and heads into the house. She was right. He is going to have to hurry if he doesn't want to be late. River has always been good at reading him. Their friendship, in essence, is more like a mother-son relationship. It seems she is always giving him advice or pointing out things that he is doing wrong.

When Mark had died, Liam thought that River would too. She had all but given up on life. At that time, it was he who became her savior. She was like a little sister to him. He had taken her under his wing and brought her back to life. However, the tables have turned somewhere down the line; now, she is like a bossy, overbearing mother. He smiles at the thought as he goes through the motions of getting dressed for tonight.

This night wouldn't be happening if it wasn't for her. She's the one who has kept him in line over this past year. He had wanted to run to Raylene and fix all her brokenness. However, it was River that urged him to give her space, give her time to heal. He now realizes that if he had followed his desires, he would have only pushed her away. But thanks to River holding him back, a friendship had formed.

Never in his life has he ever felt such a connection with someone. The smile he has been wearing all day slips away as thoughts of Lisa enter his mind. He had known Lisa most of his life. They had grown up together, went to the same school, attended the same church and Sunday school class, went to the same summer camps. Nothing could ever take away what he and Lisa shared. She was remarkable in her own way. But they never experienced this level of friendship.

It was only natural that he would marry her. You know how small towns are; it was almost expected of him. She was always his sweetheart. Everyone predicted they would marry. And they did. She was his life for as long as he had her. But then she was taken away. Losing the only love he had ever known left him feeling like he'd never be able to love again—until Raylene came along.

Although it is possible that she doesn't feel the same towards him, and what they share may never venture beyond friendship—that would be better than not having her in his life at all. He checks his reflection one last time in the mirror, then turns to leave the house. If he doesn't go now, he will surely be late, and he doesn't want to keep her waiting.

Chapter 19
Raylene

If time heals all wounds—why can't it also erase worry lines from a face? Raylene stares at her reflection in the mirror. The stress of the past year has taken a toll on her. The dark circle under her eyes have vanished, but the crows' feet and lines on her forehead seem to have gotten deeper. But, of course, maybe they have been like this all along; she just never noticed until now.

Nylah picks up the lipstick tube and waves it at her mom, "You forgot lipstick mommy."

Raylene laughs, "I don't think tonight is a lipstick kind of night, sweetie."

"But it looks so pretty—please?"

She realizes that this is a battle that could go on for hours. Therefore, giving in to her daughter would save a mound of time, "Okay, but let's choose a lighter color. This one is way too dark."

Choosing to go with a soft mauve, Raylene watches her daughter in the mirror as she applies the color to her lips. The reflection of the lights sparkles in her eyes like tiny diamonds. Tonight will be the first night in over a year that she won't be the one tucking her in at bedtime. Guilt tugs at her heart; She knows Irene is more than capable of making sure she brushes her teeth and says her prayers, but still, she doesn't want to miss those cherished moments.

"Mommy, can I put on lipstick too?"

Raylene smiles at her daughter's words.

"Please—I want to look pretty too."

Raylene pulls her daughter into her arms. "You don't need lipstick to be pretty; you are beautiful just the way you are."

Nylah giggles as she tickles her. "Let's go downstairs and wait for Liam to come." She takes her daughter's hand and heads for the stairs.

Irene turns to look at her daughter as she comes into the kitchen, "Wow! Lipstick huh?" she gives her daughter a playful smile.

"That was Nylah's idea—she wouldn't have it any other way."

"Doesn't she look beautiful, Grammy?"

"Yes, she sure does—you think Liam will approve?" Irene winks to Nylah.

"Mom! Really?" Raylene could feel her cheeks burn.

It seems that her mother has spent the past year trying to play matchmaker between her and Liam. That day at Trevor's funeral, she had intended to walk away and never speak to him again. However, legal matters arose, and she wanted someone she could trust to set her in the right direction. Ronny had been her first choice; he had pointed her to Liam. However, he could be in on trying to get the two together also.

No one seems to understand the pressure life has on her right now. Taking on college was a huge step. What better way to distract yourself from a life that seems to be falling apart than to bury yourself in studying for a career? Once she found herself free to choose the direction of her life, finishing college was her first effort in getting things back on track. However, teaching isn't her choice these days. After living in abuse for so long, she wants to help others who feel trapped in the same type of relationship. So, she's taking criminal justice to become a Victims Advocate. The people in her life need to understand her priorities, which are first her daughter, then build a career that enables her to provide for them.

How often has she told her mom that a man is not what she needs in her life right now? Those years married to an immense con artist has left her not knowing who she can trust. Irene just doesn't seem to understand; how could she? Her dad had been a wonderful husband and daddy. He had always treated her mom like a queen. No, she would never understand the magnitude of hurt that goes with being betrayed and abused by a man who is supposed to love and protect you.

"Mom! You are going on a date?" Nylah squeals in delight.

Raylene hadn't been listening to her mom and daughter's bantering, "A date? Is that what Grammy told you?" She glares over to her mother, "No, sweetie, we are going to talk business."

Irene had gone along with her idea of building a house on the backside of the property. Raylene has always thought that part of land on the lake would be a perfect spot for a home. The money that Trevor left behind and the remainder of the insurance money can make that dream a reality. Upon telling Liam of this plan, he had informed her that his cousin is an architect. A few phone calls later, and Raylene's dream home designs were underway.

"Talk business?" Irene snorted, "At this hour? Most people are home having dinner with their family; and you are going out with Liam to talk business?"

"Give it a rest mom," Raylene says as the doorbell rings. "I'll get that, we need to be going, so I can get back before late." She kisses her daughter on the forehead, "Don't stay up late sweetheart and—keep an eye on Grammy, she's talking like a crazy lady." She giggles and turns to answer the door.

"You're late," she says as she opens the door and walks out instead of inviting him in. keeping him away from Irene would be the best option.

"I was hoping you wouldn't notice," he replies as they head for the car.

"Where is your car? And whose car is this?"

"Mine died—this is a rental."

"Why did you get a rental? Is your truck dead too?"

Liam gives a laugh, "Now you're sounding like River." He closes her door and walks around, and joins her inside, "It has taken me a year to get you on a date. I was not going to have you climbing up in that old rusty truck."

She smiles over at him.

"So—what did Irene say about you *finally* going on a *real* date with me?"

"She doesn't know that this is a *real* date." She holds up her hand, "Let me explain before you get offended—she would have been all over me—getting me dressed, fixing my hair—you know, the whole *get-dolled-up* routine." She shakes her head, "I didn't want to go through all that—so—I didn't tell her."

Liam laughs, "So where does she think we are going at this hour?"

"To talk about the plans on the house."

He shakes his head in disbelief as he heads into town.

****

The evening seemed to go by so fast. Liam had planned a perfect night for the two of them. Most men at his age would have most likely gone with dinner and a movie. But not Liam. His plans were a bit unorthodox for people of their age—but it was just what she needed. First, he had taken her to the little Italian restaurant on Main

Street. Then they had driven into Blairsville to the roller rink. It has been years since she has had on a pair of skates. But she hasn't laughed and enjoyed herself that much in a very long time.

The last time she had been skating was her senior year of high school. Back then, life seemed so promising and full of hope. But little did she know at that time that would be one of the last fun, free-spirited moments of her life—until tonight. Once again, Liam seemed to know just what she needed; and he made their first date rememberable.

As they pull up to the house, she notices that the lamp is on in the living room. "Mom must still be up." She points towards the window, "Waiting on me, I'm sure."

"She wants you to fill her in on the nondate." He says as he turns in the seat to face her.

Raylene smiles over at him, "Thank you for a wonderful night. I really had fun."

"I pray it won't be the last time—I want to take you on many fun-filled dates just like tonight."

"We'll see." She teases.

He leans towards her, cups her face in his hands, and softly kisses her lips. She hadn't expected him to kiss her. So, for a moment, she only basked in the feel of his lips on hers. So many times, she had watched his lips move as he spoke, and she had wanted so much to know the taste of them. Now, here he is—his lips pressed to hers. Slowly, she parts her lips and returns the kiss.

After a few seconds, she pulls away.

"Now it is officially a real date—sealed with a kiss."

Epilogue
Two Years Later

Raylene paces back and forth on the tiny, narrow hallway backstage. Her anxiety level is through the roof. Never in her life has she ever had to speak in front of someone, and now here she is—about to face an auditorium packed to compacity. What was she thinking when she wrote that book about her story? It indeed wasn't that two years later she'd be standing here speaking to— how many?

"Liam, how many people does this place hold?"

"Compacity is two-thousand, and all the tickets sold out—so two-thousand."

"I can't speak to—no, what was I thinking? I can't do this—tell them I can't do this—I will—"

"Raylene, you got this, or should I say—God's got this." He pulls her into his arms, "You survived a horrible situation. And when you survive something like that— God gives you a message to share—so get out there and share it to all these women and men that need to hear it. I feel that when we survive something that should have killed us—we owe it to Him to tell others what we learned in the process."

Just being near this wonderful man makes her feel like she can do anything. God truly has blessed her with one of the best. But, of course, after everything she's been through, she deserves a man like Liam. Not only is he a fantastic husband, but he also took Nylah in as if she were his own. she falls in love with him even more, every time she sees the two of them together.

"Now I know why I married you," she smiles as she hugs him tightly.

"Why is that?"

"You keep me centered when I'm falling apart; and you keep reminding me of my purpose in life"

"Miss, come stand by the doorway—they are about to call you out on stage," the stagehand guy taps her arm to get her attention.

"Say a prayer for me," she whispers to Liam and walks to the stage door to await her name to be called.

"Now, give a round of applause for Raylene Geoffrey!"

She straightens her back and holds her head high as she walks to center stage and takes the microphone. "Thank You." She says to the announcer.

"And thank all of you for coming out tonight. Now, let me properly introduce myself. I'm Raylene Geoffrey— a domestic violence survivor." She smiles out over the crowd, feeling calmer than she had thought she would.

"What is domestic violence you may ask. What does it look like? And how do I know if I am in a violent relationship? I'm going to give you those answers tonight; but first, I want to give you some numbers." She takes a piece of paper that is handed to her by a stage assistant.

"1 in 4 women experience severe physical violence by an intimate partner during a lifetime. On a typical day, there are more than 20 thousand phone calls placed to domestic violence hotlines nationwide. Nearly 20 people per minute are physically abused by an intimate partner in the United States. Over the span of one year, that adds up to more than 10 million women and men—yes men get abuse too. As a matter of fact, 1 in 7 men are reported to be abused over a lifetime."

"Did you know that 1 in 15 children are exposed to intimate partner violence each year, and 90% of these children are eyewitnesses to this violence." Her voice breaks as she thinks of Nylah, "Sometimes these children get caught in the crossfires, and the damage is almost irreversible." Raylene pauses to compose herself before continuing.

"Globally as many as 38% of all murders of women are committed by intimate partners. As a matter fact—on average, more than 3 women are murdered by their intimate partners in the U.S. every day. That adds up to be an average of 1,095 women a year. Let that sink in a minute." She walks from one end of the stage to the other before continuing, "Those numbers are staggering—aren't they?"

Empathetic groans echo through the crowd.

"Now just imagine this," she leans out over the edge of the stage, "Most cases of domestic violence are *never reported* to the police. The numbers I just gave you are based on what has been reported—and they are astonishing. How large would that number be if everyone reported?"

"Now let's answer the question I asked at the beginning, what is domestic violence?" Raylene pauses to glance at Liam standing just off stage; she smiles as he gives her an encouraging wink. "Domestic violence is the willful intimidation, physical assault, battery, sexual assault, and/or abusive behavior perpetrated by one intimate partner against another in an effort to maintain power and control over the other."

"Let me tell you what that looks like. I used to say things like, he doesn't hit me much—only when I don't do things the way he wants them done. Besides, he's only hit me three or four times over nine years. Abuse isn't just physical hitting or beating; and it's not always easy to determine in the early stages of a relationship. As a matter of fact, the abuser usually seems wonderful and perfect initially. But unfortunately, that doesn't last for long; the abuser gradually becomes more aggressive and controlling as the relationship continues. One day everything seems perfect, then the next—it's as if you are with a stranger."

"Abuse may begin with behaviors that may easily be dismissed or downplayed. Behaviors like, name calling, threats, possessiveness, or distrust. The abuser may apologize profusely for their actions or try to convince you that they do these things out of love or care. However, violence and control always intensify over time, despite the apologies. What may start out as something that was first believed to be harmless, like, wanting you to spend all their time with them because they love you so much; escalates into extreme control and abuse, like, threatening to kill or hurt you or others if you speak to family or friends."

"Domestic violence doesn't always end when the victim escapes the abuser or tries to end the relationship or seeks help. Often it intensifies because the abuser feels a loss of control over the victim. The abuser frequently continues to stalk, harass, threaten, and try to control the victim. In fact, the victim is often in the most danger directly following the escape of the relationship or seeking help. Twenty percent of homicides are victims with restraining orders who were murdered within two days of obtaining the order. Thirty-three percent are murdered within the first month."

"In my situation, it is true—he didn't hit me too often; but he was always telling me I couldn't do anything right. I was never allowed to visit with my mom, nor she with me. I even had to sneak and have conversations with the neighbor. He controlled the money; I had to ask if I needed anything; and then I had to do things to *earn* the money he gave me. Numerous times I was told I was a bad mother; and was even intimidated with guns and knives. The list goes on and on, until one day I got tired of it, and I wanted out. But I didn't know who to turn to for help; so, I attempted to do it on my own—it almost cost me my life."

"I was stabbed numerous times. Bleeding profusely, I ran from the house to a convenience store nearby. Upon regaining consciousness, I found myself in a hospital, and—he had gone on the run with my daughter. Several months passed before I got her back."

Raylene lightens the mood with a soft laugh, "I'm not telling you this to scare you into staying in an abusive relationship. The truth is, bringing an end to the abuse is not a matter of the victim choosing to leave; it's a matter of the victim being able to safely *escape* their abuser. And there are people out there to help make this possible. That's my main reason for being here today—to teach you the signs of abuse; and to point you in the direction of help out of it."

She finishes the speech by informing the audience on places to find the haven of escape. Then, as the standing ovation fills the auditorium, she exits the stage and almost runs into Liam's arms. "I did it," she whispers as he squeezes her tightly.

"Now I remember why I married *you.*" He smiles down at her.

"Why is that?"

"Because you are absolutely amazing."

*Statics cited on: https://ncadv.org/STATISTICS

Note from the author

If you or someone you know is in an abusive relationship, there is help. Start by calling the National Domestic Violence Hotline at 1-800-799-SAFE (7233) now.

ABOUT THE AUTHOR

Karen Pless Gaines lives in Northeast Georgia with her husband and two children, and grandson. After living in abusive relationships for many years, her goal is to provide victims with the information they need to get help. Unfortunately, this was information that she was not made aware of until it was almost too late.

Find me on:

www.facebook.com/authorkpgaines

Instagram: @authorkpgaines

Web: karenplessgaines.weebly.com

TikTok: @karenplessgaines